"Someone wants you out of the picture," Myles said.

Kenzie's face went white, and she slowly slipped to the floor, as though her legs would not hold her one more second. "What do you mean?"

Myles did not want to have this conversation. But she had to know. Or she'd up and leave and be in more danger than ever before.

Oh Lord, I've really messed this whole situation up. But YOU know I only want to protect Kenzie. Please show me how to make her understand. I haven't been doing a good job of that lately. Give me Your words to explain everything to her.

When Myles glanced back at Kenzie, he saw that her face was still turned up to him in expectant hope. She was actually soft and tender, a far cry from the feisty redhead she often portrayed. He couldn't decide who he liked better, sweet or spicy Kenzie. Both fascinated him.

D0804602

LIZ JOHNSON

After graduating from Northern Arizona University in Flagstaff with a degree in public relations, Liz Johnson set out to work in the Christian publishing industry, which was her lifelong dream. In 2006, she got her wish when she accepted a publicity position at a major trade book publisher. While working as a publicist in the industry, she decided to pursue her other dream— being an author. Along the way to having her novel published, she wrote articles for several magazines.

Liz lives in Colorado Springs, Colorado, where she enjoys theater, ice skating, volunteering in her church's bookstore and making frequent trips to Arizona to dote on her nephew and three nieces. She loves stories of true love with happy endings. *The Kidnapping of Kenzie Thorn* is her first novel.

Liz Johnson

The
KIDNAPPING *of*
KENZIE THORN

Steeple
Hill®

Published by Steeple Hill Books™

STEEPLE HILL BOOKS

Steeple
Hill®

ISBN-13: 978-0-373-44348-2

THE KIDNAPPING OF KENZIE THORN

www.SteepleHill.com

Printed in U.S.A.

But the eyes of the Lord are on those who fear him, on those whose hope is in his unfailing love...We wait in hope for the Lord; he is our help and our shield.

—Psalms 33:18, 20

To Mom and Dad.
You are amazing parents, cheerleaders
and most of all friends. Thanks for setting
an example of loving God.

To the rest of the Johnson/Whitson Clan:
Micah, Beth, Hannah, John and all the kids.
Thank you for helping me leap those first obligatory
hurdles and making me laugh along the way.
I'm so thankful to be part of this family.

And to my Monday night writing buddy
Jessica Barnes and my first editor Kelly Blewett;
the first draft (and every subsequent version) of this
story would never have seen the light of day without
you both. I treasure our friendship.

A special thanks to Elizabeth Mazer, who took a
chance on me and saw something worth her time.
I'm a better writer because of you.

ONE

Mackenzie Thorn looked up just in time to see two men walk into her classroom. One of them, a guard, nodded at his coworker stationed inside the door, and kept his hand at the elbow of the taller man beside him. This man, clad in an orange jumpsuit sporting the initials ODOC—Oregon Department of Corrections—swaggered into the classroom, head held high, windswept brown hair falling over his collar. The intensity of his blue eyes struck Kenzie immobile for a moment as they approached.

"Ms. Thorn," the guard began.

Kenzie shook her head to clear her thoughts before holding up one index finger to the guard. "Just a moment, please." Turning to the two men sitting at the first table on her right, she said, "Mr. Ramirez, Mr. Chen, please pass out workbooks to everyone." The two men began their task while she moved to meet her new student.

"This is Myles Parsons. The superintendent's office said to put him in this class."

The guard made no apologies for bringing in a new student five weeks into their six-week GED session. Decrees from Superintendent JB Ryker's office were law inside these walls. The inmate would just have to try to keep up.

The man's piercing blue eyes bore into her face, seeming to study every crevice. She knew for a fact that her face was not that interesting. Mr. Parsons's face, on the other hand, was well worth studying. The crooked bridge of his nose had been broken at least once, but the imperfection was intriguing rather than off-putting. His wide mouth and pink lips pulled into a smirk, exposing his arrogance. Running thick fingers through his shaggy brown hair, he continued staring back at her, something few of her other students had ever dared to do.

Suddenly she realized how incredibly inappropriate she was being and ripped her gaze away from his handsome face. "Welcome to our GED prep class, Mr. Parsons."

"So you're Ms. Thorn?"

"Yes, I am. You seem surprised."

"I am." The man certainly did not mince words. "I expected someone more…" He stretched to his full height, which was at least a foot taller than her. "The way the others talk, I expected someone more intimidating."

Despite her skittering pulse, she quirked the corner of her mouth into a partial grin. "Trust me, Mr. Parsons. My tests are plenty intimidating. You may take a seat now. Third row on the left." Effectively dismissing him, she turned to the rest of the class and began teaching the basic fraction lesson.

Myles Parsons gazed at Ms. Mackenzie Thorn. Obviously frustrated by her wild, curly hair, she shoved it behind her ears, giving herself streaks of white where the chalk from her fingers lingered in her curls.

Her passion for the mundane principles of fractions astounded him. Her voice, like a melody, rose and fell as she singsonged through adding and subtracting the tricky numbers.

He shook his head to clear away the distractions of her intense gray eyes. He chastised himself for his own bad luck to end up inside these walls. Her pretty face wouldn't be enough to make his current mission worth it.

Somehow, he'd let his FBI supervisor, Special Agent in Charge Nathan—Nate—Andersen, talk him into taking this assignment. An assignment that could be summed up in two words: Kenzie Thorn.

When Nate received a tip two weeks before that the governor's granddaughter was in danger working inside the Oregon State Prison Complex at Evergreen, Myles had wondered about the validity of the tip. But Nate believed it, and he'd assigned an agent to the inside to protect her. As the youngest special agent stationed in the office, and one of the few without a family, Myles was the obvious pick to go behind bars to protect Kenzie.

Protect her from what, he wasn't sure.

But as long as he was on this mission, he'd keep an eye on her. He'd do his job and do it well.

Kenzie—Ms. Thorn, as he was going to have to think of her—turned around at the front of the class and flicked another streak of white through her hair, rambling on about finding the lowest common denominator. His mouth quirked up at the corners of its own accord at her spunky head bob, and he had to fake a sneeze in order to keep from laughing out loud.

"You're smiling awfully hard for a man who is five weeks behind the rest of the class, Mr. Parsons." Ms. Thorn's voice was soft, and she leaned closer to him, suddenly at his side. She smelled like citrus, like lemon and lime mixed together. Relishing the crisp scent in a room full of mostly unwashed bodies, he looked up into her stormy gray eyes. A row of freckles at the top of the bridge of her nose softened her hard glare, and he physically had to fight a smirk in response to her childlike cuteness.

One thing was quite certain. She wasn't going to erase his smile standing this close to him.

An intriguing contradiction, her piercing eyes and gentle face tempted Myles to turn this exchange into a flirtation. Shoving those thoughts away, he focused on the mission, knowing he had to keep his mind alert for any signs she might be in danger.

Finally, the class ended, and Kenzie took a moment to let her head rest on her desk, trying to clear her mind from the terrible day she'd just had. The day started with Cory Johns, one of her favorite students, cheating on his third and final try at the GED exam, forcing her to fail him. Any hope for a change in his life after his release went in the trash with his exam.

The next class brought her new student, Myles Parsons, whose cocky smirk and arrogance made her bristle every time she looked in his direction. He raised his hand to answer almost every question she asked, and even worse, he was always right!

Eyes closed and forehead still leaning on her arm draped over the papers littering her desk, Kenzie took the opportunity to pray for her students.

God, please give me the words to reach these men. To give them some hope and skills for when they are released. I pray for the families that are eagerly waiting for their return. And, Lord, I pray specifically for Cory Johns. I pray that he will find another way to earn his GED and support his family. And I ask that You give me a special dose of patience for my new student. Please help his attitude to change toward me and this class. Thank You for Your many good gifts. In Your name, Amen.

Just as she dragged her head from its resting spot, a noise in the doorway caught her attention. A handsome man with sleek silver hair filled the entire doorway.

"Mac!" she cried, jumping up from her seat and throwing herself into the man's waiting embrace. She clung tightly to him as he almost squeezed the breath out of her. "What are you doing here? I wasn't expecting you until tomorrow."

"You know how it is." He chuckled, a smile spreading over his face. "Sometimes the governor's schedule changes." He gave her another quick squeeze before stepping back to really look at her.

His gray eyes, so much like her own, assessed her carefully and he frowned. "You look tired. Is this position too much for you?"

Kenzie resisted the urge to roll her eyes. He said the same thing every time he saw her. "I've been here for two years. I'm doing okay."

"Are you taking care of yourself?"

"Of course." She looped her arm through Mac's and smiled into his loving face. "I've missed you, Grandpa." She rarely called Mac "Grandpa," and since he was elected governor nearly six years before, she could count on one hand the number of times she had done so. But today she needed to be reminded that she was loved by her father's father, the man who had loved her as a daughter, ever since she lost her parents all those years ago.

Mac squeezed her tightly to his side and kissed the top of her head. "Sweet pea, you have no idea how much we miss you in Salem. I can pull some strings to get you a position at a school there. You'd make a wonderful kindergarten teacher. This place is rough. It's not good for you."

"It's okay. I'm okay. They need me, and to tell you the truth, I think I need them, too." Kenzie smiled and snuggled a little closer to his side. Mac had always been able to right the wrongs in her life, protect her from the boogeyman, dry her tears. He was larger than life when she was a child, and his presence today almost wiped away thoughts of concern over her new student.

She looked around Mac's arm and spotted his usual entourage. "Harry. Buzz." She nodded at each of the men standing just inside the doorway. Harry was built like a bulldozer and Buzz like a long-distance runner. They were part of the best security detail in the state, and Kenzie had grown fond of them through the years, as they protected Mac. "Candace." She acknowledged Mac's personal aide, a tall blonde standing beside Buzz.

Candace looked up from the notes in her daily planner. "Good afternoon, Kenzie." She offered a brief smile, then returned to keeping Mac on schedule.

"Well, you'd best show me around your classroom." Mac's voice was gruff, but held a grin.

"Sure. There's not much to show really. We have tables where the students sit. Our bookshelf is pretty meager, but the prison library has a good selection that I sometimes assign for additional reading, for those that need the practice to prepare for the exam. And of course, my desk."

As Kenzie pointed out the tables, sparse bookshelves and her own desk, Mac walked around the room, glancing at the mathematic posters, the only decoration on the gray walls. He glanced twice at a particularly colorful formula, hand-drawn, on a large white poster board, but he didn't comment.

"How's the program?" he finally said.

"It's wonderful. Since you authorized this pilot program two years ago, we've had more than two hundred inmates earn GEDs. We have almost a two-thirds pass rate. You don't have to worry about us right now. But maybe—"

"You're a good kid, Mackenzie Thorn." He cut her off before she could confess that she was hoping the state legislature might be able to allocate more funds. Distracted by his use of her full name, she forgot what she was going to say. No one called her or Mac by their shared first name. After complications with their first and only pregnancy, Kenzie's parents had decided to pass the family name down through their daughter, even if it was a man's name. She'd worn it proudly, always going by Kenzie to avoid confusion.

Now she smiled wider in response to Mac's compliment. Could he tell how much she loved teaching these men? Could he read in her eyes how much it broke her heart when they chose to give up, rather than fight for the skills that could lead to a new life?

A noise in the doorway made her turn. JB Ryker, the prison superintendent and an old friend of Mac's, limped into the classroom, nudging Harry and Buzz aside. His knee had been injured during the Vietnam War, and when it rained he often needed the aid of a cane to manage the slick cement halls of the prison.

"Macky, you ol' dog." Kenzie cringed inwardly. She always hated it when JB called her grandfather "Macky." He was the only one who could get away with it, and Mac never seemed to mind. But she still hated it.

She also hated the way his lip curled up, like a back-alley used-car salesman. Something about him always made her skin crawl.

"Why the early trip?" JB said.

Shaking hands with his old friend, Mac said, "I have a meeting tomorrow at the capital that couldn't be rescheduled."

"Must be tough being the governor."

Mac just grinned. He'd taught Kenzie to hold her tongue in situations like this, where there was no right answer. If only she could do as he taught.

"It's certainly not easy, Superintendent," she retorted. A sharp glance from Mac made her bite her tongue to keep from saying anything else.

JB ignored her comment. "What do you think of the

place? I'm sure Kenzie has kept you up-to-date on the success of the program."

"Yes, she was just filling me in. It seems to be working well. If the statistics remain this high, we may move forward with expanding the program to the other state prisons sooner than expected."

For an instant, JB looked like he'd swallowed his tongue. But he swiftly recovered, putting on his famous poker face. "That's wonderful. How soon do you think?"

"I think we can start moving forward now. It should take us just a couple of months to get things in place in the other prisons, as we have such a strong example to work from with the test program here at the Evergreen complex."

"That's wonderful, Mac!" Kenzie's smile was so wide it almost hurt her cheeks. With the expanded program, the state might be able to set aside a little more for her own classes. She opened her mouth to ask Mac just that, but stopped herself when she looked at Ryker. He'd warned her not to discuss the budget with Mac, but sometimes she had to physically restrain herself from asking for just a little more money. When Candace called to him, Mac hurried across the room, grabbing the cell phone she held.

Kenzie looked at JB's surly face and wondered if he might answer some of her questions. He hated talking budget. "We don't talk budgets, except at budget meetings," he had said on her first day. "And we don't discuss budgets with anyone outside of prison, including family. Including your grandfather. If Mac increased the budget at your request, his opponents could claim he gave you preferential treatment. That could damage his chances in another run for the governor's office." His hard glare had been stern, almost cruel, and she shivered even now at the mere possibility that she could hinder Mac's chances at reelection.

With Mac on the other side of the room, she seized what might be her only chance to talk with JB alone. Regardless of her apprehension toward JB, this would help her students and other prisoners.

"If the program is ready to expand already, do you think the state legislature might be able to increase funding for us just a bit? I worked out some figures, and raising our budget by just fifteen percent could increase the number of students we can accommodate by over twenty-five percent." JB stared back at her blankly. Keeping her voice low, she plowed on. "I'm planning on petitioning the legislature next month for an increase in the budget for the next fiscal year."

JB's face twisted slightly. "What's wrong?" Kenzie asked.

"Oh, nothing," he said gruffly, his eyes darting quickly in Mac's direction.

"What's going on?"

JB sighed. "I know Mac doesn't want to bring this up, but this governor's race is getting sticky. Things are being said by his opponent."

Suddenly Mac was back by her side, and she turned to look at him, praying that things were not going wrong. "What is your opponent saying, Mac?" He shook his head, but she squeezed his hand tightly. "Tell me what's going on."

"Claudia Suarez has purchased some advertising that makes me out to be something of a crook. She says I haven't been completely responsible with the state's budget."

"But it's not true! Just tell them that it's not true." Tears filled Kenzie's eyes, and she knuckled them away angrily.

"It's not that easy, sweetheart. The voters are going to believe what they believe. But this could be a closer race than we thought."

Men in orange jumpsuits suddenly began filing into the room, taking their assigned seats. The men nearest to her sat staring at their hands folded on the table. None of them said anything or looked at her, Mac or JB. Taking advantage of the men's lack of attention, she blinked rapidly and rubbed black smudges of mascara onto her fingers from her bottom eyelids.

"I have another class to teach, Mac, but I'll see you tonight, right? We'll finish talking about this?"

He shot a glance at Candace, who checked her calendar then nodded. "Of course. I'll take you out for a steak after you finish with this class. There's nothing to worry about. I've got it all under control." He squeezed her shoulder, winked at her, then followed JB toward the door. Somehow, that was all it took to reassure her that everything was right with the world.

"What looks good?" Mac said, sitting across the table from Kenzie that night.

"Maybe the prime rib with steamed vegetables."

"Hmm. That does sound good. But it's been a long time since I've had a good T-bone and baked potato."

"Nana hasn't made you any lately?" Kenzie asked. It seemed a bit strange for Mac to not have a good steak and potatoes regularly. Her grandmother was a wonderful cook and had created an amazing pineapple-chipotle marinade that Mac loved.

When Kenzie was growing up in Mac and Nana's home, Nana loved to cook for the three of them. Each evening meal was a special event, with delicious food and close conversation around the dining-room table. Those nights provided the stability that Kenzie craved after her parents' deaths. At the age of five she had struggled to understand, to accept what was really happening. Her father, Mackenzie Thorn II, was an avid pilot. He and her mother, Grace, loved to fly together, traveling the country.

It had only taken one plane crash to leave her an orphan. And in Kenzie's childhood mind, it only took two of her grandmother's meals to know that she wouldn't have to be alone again. Mac and Nana took her into their home and loved her as their own daughter through grade school, high school, college and beyond.

"We've both been very busy lately," Mac said in response to Kenzie's question.

"Where is Nana?" It seemed strange to Kenzie that Nana would choose not to accompany Mac on a trip.

Just then the waiter arrived to take their orders—and just as quickly disappeared.

When it appeared that Mac had forgotten the question, she asked again. "Where's Nana? I haven't seen her in almost six weeks." Living in Evergreen, close to the prison—but a two-hour drive from Salem—Kenzie often missed seeing her grandmother regularly.

"Oh, she…she decided not to come on this trip. It's mostly just meetings and election items on my agenda. Your grand-mother would have been bored, tagging along on this trip." Mac cleared his throat and adjusted his silverware. He seemed a bit stiff, oddly uncertain of himself.

He was probably worried about his opponent, Claudia Suarez.

Kenzie reached out and covered Mac's weathered hand with her own, much smaller one. "You're thinking about Claudia Suarez, aren't you?"

Mac looked a little bit guilty. "I'm afraid so. I can't stop wondering what her advertising lies will do to my election."

"But she can't just lie and get away with it, can she?"

Mac's broad shoulders beneath his suit jacket rose and fell with his sigh. "No, she can't outright lie. But there's nothing stopping her from twisting the truth and making it look like I'm not doing my job, or have taken advantage of my position."

"But you're the best thing that's ever happened to the state of Oregon! Just think about how much this prison education reform is helping the inmates and their families on the outside."

A broad grin spread across Mac's lips. "Thanks for the support, honey." He squeezed her hand, and in that moment, Kenzie was never more proud to carry his name.

"Now," he said, suddenly looking stern, "your grandmother tells me that you met a young man."

Kenzie burst into laughter, her cheeks turned a bit red as she answered Mac's questions about her virtually nonexistent dating life. The only men she had time for these days were her students.

Like Myles Parsons.

Something about the inmate intrigued her. His arrogant smirk and cocky attitude warned her that he could be trouble if she wasn't careful. But the unsteady rhythm of her heart during their first encounter hinted that he already affected her more than she cared to admit.

Mac's brow wrinkled. "You know, if you moved to Salem, there would be more single men for your consideration. And I can guarantee you a position at Northgate Academy. I went to college with the headmaster there."

Kenzie smiled and patted Mac's hand across the table. This wasn't the first time—today—they had discussed her leaving the prison. "I do love kids," she began, before she was interrupted by the waiter delivering their meals. She bowed her head and offered a quick, silent prayer of thanksgiving.

God, thank You for this food. And please soften Mac's heart toward You. In Your name—Oh! And please take care of the men in my classes, and help them to follow the rules and stay out of trouble with the guards. Especially Myles.

The moment she lifted her head, Kenzie saw Mac's knowing smile. "I know you love kids. So why not work with them? Think how wonderful it would be, being close to your grandmother and me."

"Well… it would be nice to be closer to you. But what about these inmates? They deserve to have someone believe in them. Why shouldn't it be me?"

"But why does it have to be you? There are plenty of other qualified teachers that could take your place."

Kenzie tried to keep the sting of those words from showing on her face. How could she explain how much she loved working with the men at the prison—teaching them, offering them hope beyond the walls of the prison? Would another teacher pray for the inmates, care for them as she did? She took a bite of her prime rib and chewed slowly on the succulent meat, buying some time.

"I like children, but I really love my job right now. I'm not going to leave."

"But think of the pay raise and the budget for your classroom in a private school like that."

Kenzie looked directly into Mac's gray eyes and said, "No. I'm not leaving."

Mac's shoulders slumped as he shoveled a chunk of steak into his mouth, his whole face morose.

"So tell me about the campaign. What have you been up to, other than dealing with Claudia Suarez?" As she'd hoped, Mac was easily distracted with the details of the campaign. He quickly obliged, falling into stories from the electoral trail.

As he regaled her with tales, Kenzie's mind drifted for just a minute to another man in her life. Blue eyes and a handsome face flashed through her thoughts. She fought the smile that Myles's memory brought and had to physically shake her head to clear away any thoughts of him.

This night was about her relationship with Mac, not some strangely intriguing new inmate.

TWO

Two days later, Kenzie sighed softly as she waited for the guard to open the front gate far enough to pull her maroon sedan into the bus barn inside the prison walls. She slipped the gear shift into Park, turned off the engine, but remained seated behind the wheel.

Her stomach felt like it was tied in knots, and she took two cleansing breaths. But the uneasy feeling remained.

Usually she only felt this way the day of the GED exam, which was still three days away for her most advanced class. Forcing herself to be honest, Kenzie admitted to herself that today she feared facing a set of piercing blue eyes and an arrogant smirk. Oh, she had really done it this time. She had crossed the line of professionalism that was to be strictly adhered to at the prison, for her own safety, and now she had to face up to her mistake.

Leaning her forehead on her steering wheel and closing her eyes, in her mind she replayed the scene from the day before.

"Great work today, guys." She took a sip of water from the cup on her desk as the men shuffled papers into a pile for her to collect after they left. "Now, don't forget that we have a review of the math section tomorrow and an English review the next day. The following class I'll be taking your questions, so make sure you have plenty to keep us busy. And the next class—the following week—is your test."

Per their usual, the men mumbled unintelligible responses.

Larry, her usual guard, stepped forward from his location just inside the door of the room and the men began lining up to exit. Kenzie started erasing the chalkboard, white dust billowing around her head.

"Ms. Thorn."

She jumped at the sound of her name. Larry stood on the other side of her desk.

"Yes?"

"Superintendent Ryker wants to meet with Inmate Parsons. He just radioed that he's been held up at another meeting and will be here in just a few minutes. He said to have Parsons wait here for him. I'll be right here at the door if you need anything."

"That's fine. Since he was late today, it'll give us a chance to make sure he's ready for the exam in a few days." As the guard motioned to Parsons to return to his seat, she knew she hadn't spoken the whole truth. The whole truth was that Myles Parsons was more ready to take the GED than any other student she had taught in her two years at the prison. He probably could have passed the exam his first day in her class.

Larry moved to the open doorway, standing half in the hallway, leaving Kenzie and Myles in relative privacy.

"Good lesson today," Myles said from his seat at a table, his tone serious. But his eyes and wicked smirk mocked her from his semirecumbent position.

She heard Mac's advice to not respond when there was no good counter, but ignored it, blurting, "You have no idea— You just don't get— What is your problem?" She charged at him, fists clenched at her sides. She certainly had no intention of hitting him, but his one little comment and snide sneer riled her beyond reason.

Just as she reached the table where he sat, he stood. Forced to crane her neck just to look at his chin, her anger boiled hotter. How dare he try to intimidate her with his size? With those broad shoulders and muscular arms?

One call to Larry would have Myles in solitary confinement for a week.

Only one other inmate had ever tried to intimidate her. That was well over a year ago. That time she had crumbled, calling for the guard on duty, having the inmate permanently removed from her class. Fearing that the other inmates in her classes would think they could overrun her, Kenzie had grown braver, stronger. She had read somewhere that kindness could be mistaken for weakness. She let her students know right away after that incident that that was not the case with her. But now she was faced with another inmate who wouldn't back down. She should have been angry or frightened, but she wasn't. Inexplicably, she felt safe with him. Oh, he might infuriate her, but for some reason, she felt he'd never hurt her. Was she a fool to trust him so much?

Those terrible, beautiful blue eyes never looked away, never broke eye contact as Myles put his hands around her fists and held them gently.

"I meant it as a compliment," he whispered. "The polite thing to do would be to say 'thank you.'"

She should have wrenched her hands from his, stepped back, put at least three feet between them. Instead she took a tiny step toward him, closer to the strength he exuded.

Finally able to look away from his hypnotic eyes, she noticed a bruise forming around his right cheekbone. "What happened?" she instantly demanded. Of their own volition, the fingers of her right hand gently probed his cheek, feeling minor swelling. Was this from an inmate? Or worse, a guard?

That offending smirk returned as he gently pushed her

away. Just then JB and Larry had charged into the classroom, pushing desks out of their way as they appraised Myles.

Today Kenzie hung her head low, still too embarrassed to exit her car. While nothing really tangible happened between her and Myles, they both knew that rules had been broken. She was to have no physical contact with any inmate. And she certainly wasn't supposed to enjoy the feel of his hands briefly holding hers.

He simultaneously irritated and intrigued her. Along with her trust in him came more emotions than she wanted to own up to at the moment. Was she crazy? She didn't even know what he was convicted of. How could she think that he was safe, that she would be safe with him?

God, why does my heart skip a beat every time this man, who is so clearly off-limits, comes around? she prayed. *I just don't understand what's wrong with me! He's an inmate, and yet I can't help the way my stomach drops to my toes when I see him. He makes me so angry, but he makes me feel so safe. Please take these feelings away from me. I don't want them anymore.*

Glancing at her watch, she realized she was already five minutes late for her first class of the day. "See what you made me do, you…you…blue-eyed man," she grumbled to herself as she hurried from the car to the security checkpoint. "You made me late!"

The rest of the morning and the first part of the afternoon sped by in a blur.

When three o'clock arrived, she said goodbye to her second class and began preparing for her advanced class, which would arrive in just thirty minutes. *Myles* would arrive in just thirty minutes. Her heart gave a telltale flutter at the thought of his grin. That sometimes-teasing, sometimes-kind, sometimes-devastating grin.

Devastating? Are you kidding? Kenz, what is wrong with

you? Too many romantic daydreams. Get your head in the ball game!

Pushing aside her own inner monologue, Kenzie began doing the physical chores to prepare for the class. Scooting chairs behind desks and wiping off chalkboards required little mental activity, and for the time being she thought it might be best to wipe everything from her mind.

Especially Myles Parsons.

But her heart betrayed her when the inmates in her third class began walking into the classroom. It leapt excitedly, as she anticipated seeing Myles's face. She watched each man intently as he entered. Nineteen orange jumpsuits, nineteen men, nineteen faces. But no piercing blue eyes.

Where could he be, just a few days before the exam?

A body slammed Myles out of line as he walked toward Ms. Thorn's classroom. He had managed to maneuver his way to the very end of the line. If he was completely honest with himself, which he really did not want to be at that moment, he had finagled his way to the end of the line of prisoners, hoping to have some opportunity to connect with Ms. Thorn.

As he hoped every day during class. Only because of the mission, of course.

He knew the rules, knew that breaking them meant solitary confinement. And while he had no desire to spend a week alone in a hole—that would defeat the purpose of keeping an eye on Kenzie—neither could he deny the strange effect she had on him when they were in the same room. He knew he needed to keep his contact with her in check, but she made it awfully difficult to keep his mind on his assignment.

Now bright spots flashed before Myles's closed eyes. He rested his aching head against the block wall, leaning the rest of his body heavily there, too. He felt like a bulldozer had just rammed him into a brick wall.

Peeking out of the corner of his eye, he saw that the rest of his class was already in the classroom along with the new guard. He and the bulldozer were alone in the hallway.

Venturing a peek at the other man's uniform shirt and brown pants, Myles mumbled, "Did I do something wrong, boss?"

The guard—what was his name?—Whitestall, didn't say anything for several seconds. He just smacked his open palm with the enormous flashlight that doubled as a nightstick.

"Do you think I'm stupid, Parsons?"

"No, sir!" Myles jumped. Whatever this was, it was not going to go in his favor.

"Did you think I wouldn't notice you cozying up to the teacher?"

Myles bit his lip and kept his mouth shut. Nothing he said would improve this situation. He wanted to know what Whitestall was after, what he was trying to hunt out. Silence was usually the best provocateur.

"You know that if I turn you in to the superintendent for inappropriate conduct with a female state employee, you'll be spending the next six months in solitary."

"Yes, sir." It was best to agree with anything the guard said, though six months seemed a bit extreme. Likely he was just trying to intimidate Myles.

"Do you want to spend six months in solitary?"

"No, sir."

"I didn't think so." Whitestall leered and let out a long, putrid breath. Sweat beaded on his jaw, and his greasy hair fell in front of his beady eyes. He stopped beating his flashlight against his palm for a moment. "I've seen you and Ms. Thorn in her classroom, when you think I'm not watching. The way you look at her—sidle up to her. You want to get closer, don't you? You wish you were outside these walls, so you could *really* get to know her."

Myles was stunned. How could he possibly respond? Silence was his only hope, so he bit the inside of his cheek viciously to keep quiet.

"I knew it," Whitestall snarled. "I can see it in your eyes. You'll be in solitary for a year if I turn you in." A slow, cruel smile shaped his lips. "But…I might be willing to help you. Get you what you want and let you have a little fun with her…if you do something for me. You've got nothing to lose now."

Where was this going? "What did you have in mind, sir?"

The guard held up what looked like a silver car key.

"It's simple enough, really. I want you to make her disappear. For good."

The silver car key in Myles's pocket poked his leg as he stretched out on the back floor of Kenzie's car. He ran a hand over his new jeans, supplied by Whitestall, and tipped his head, angling for a view out of the enormous windows in the bus barn. Late afternoon, he guessed.

It would probably be at least a couple more hours before she would leave for the day. Whitestall had told him that she usually didn't leave until it was dark.

That meant he had some time to make plans and think through this crazy turn of events.

He'd never even considered that this would be a possibility of the job. That he'd be forced to kidnap his mission. To be honest, he hadn't even been convinced she was truly in danger. But he knew better now. Someone wanted her dead.

Number one rule of protection: Don't let your assignment die.

As soon as they made it out of the prison, he could take care of that.

Rule number two: Find out who wants your charge dead, and why.

Certainly Whitestall wasn't the man in charge, but Myles at least had a good place to start. That guard could and would point him in the right direction.

While he was investigating, he needed to stash Ms. Thorn in a safe location. There was an FBI safe house less than a hundred and fifty miles away. That would work. Get her there, touch base later with his supervisor. Then the really exciting stuff started—following the clues from Whitestall to the perpetrators. Who knew where that trail might lead?

He loved the unknown about this job.

Normally, at this point in a case he'd be running scenarios, figuring out angles, making plans. Yet, for some reason, his mind kept wandering back to his last interaction with Ms. Thorn.

He really had meant to compliment her on the lesson the day before. She was an excellent teacher and had a great rapport with the inmates. She provided easily understood instructions and taught with so much passion that it seemed possible she could teach the entire prison.

But he just hadn't been able to keep that smirk off his face. The force of habit was too strong. He'd used it all his life to keep the people around him at a distance. And it came in especially handy in prison. It was much easier to be guarded by other men when he kept himself emotionally removed from the situation.

As soon as Kenzie had seen his sneer, he recognized the fire in her eyes and flare of her nostrils that told him she was spitting mad. And his immediate reaction was to soothe her. But by grasping her hands, he hadn't soothed her, he'd crossed the line. He knew it. She knew it.

So why had she stepped closer to him?

He wanted the chance to look into her eyes today. To see if

she was still mad, or had forgiven him that insolent smirk. He was strangely surprised that her opinion of him really did matter. Her funny little smile—well, that was just an added bonus.

Kenzie Thorn was a spunky woman. A very attractive spunky woman.

But for the moment, she was just a job. And completing his assignment for the bureau was more important than seeing her smile or smelling her citrus scent.

Besides, as soon as she got into the car tonight, any affinity they shared would be demolished. When she crawled behind the wheel after her final class, he was going to have to threaten her life. At least make her believe that she was in danger.

Wrapping his hand firmly around the tiny blade that Whitestall had given him, he tried not to focus on the fear he knew he was going to cause.

No matter what, it was better him than someone who might like scaring Kenzie, who might really hurt her.

Suddenly the truth of that slammed into him, almost stealing his breath. *God, thank You for putting me here and not someone who would be willing to hurt her. Please keep her calm as we make our way toward the safe house tonight, and give her understanding when I can finally tell her about this assignment. I ask for wisdom as I investigate the people behind this plot against Kenzie. Lord, I pray, too, for her family, who will be frightened beyond belief. Please guide me, Lord, on my mission to protect her.*

He mouthed an "amen," not daring to say it aloud, just in case Whitestall or someone else had bugged the car. He couldn't take any chances that they would catch on to him before he had Kenzie tucked away in the safe house.

They'd make it out of the prison. And he'd find the people behind this plot. He'd make sure that she never had to worry about them again.

* * *

Kenzie sighed as she collected the last of her papers to be graded the next day, particularly tired after an extra late night of grading. Myles had never showed up for class. Immediately, her mind jumped to the sight of the yellowish bruise around his eye when he'd first entered her class the previous day. Could he have been beaten up? Was he seriously injured?

Suddenly breathing heavily, she shoved the papers haphazardly into her desk drawer and headed toward the infirmary. The evening nurse, Jayne, was always kind and would tell her if Myles was in there. But how could she ask about him without seeming too interested?

"Please don't let him be hurt," she whispered toward the ceiling. "If You see fit, please keep him safe and healthy."

Kenzie slid to a stop at the window where the middle-aged nurse should have been. But no one was there. There was no point in waiting around for Jayne or someone else to show up. It could be hours.

Turning around dejectedly, she trotted toward the security checkpoint. Having learned to navigate security efficiently, she quickly flashed her ID tag and bustled out the door, toward her car. Shivering as a sturdy breeze cooled off the evening air, she picked up her speed.

The night fell on her, closing around her. The ominous spotlights illuminating the prison yard did little to make her feel safe. Shadows in the bus barn spooked her as she flung open her car door, threw in her purse and jumped behind the wheel. The ignition turned over and the engine purred to life as she shoved the lock down.

Putting a hand over her heart, she felt the solid thuds as it raced. She took a deep breath trying to calm her jitters. She was almost never frightened inside the prison complex. What would cause her to be so scared tonight?

Deep breath in. Hold it. Let it out.

She pulled in front of the gate and waited for the guard reading the magazine to wave her through. He barely looked up long enough to punch the button that made the gate squeak loudly, then grind slowly open.

She waved back at him, but even in the glow of the light from the guard station, she felt shrouded in darkness. Out on the road on her way back into Evergreen, the darkness didn't abate. In fact, it started to close in even tighter around her. Her hands shook as they clung to the wheel and the hairs on the back of her neck stood on end, as though someone was breathing right behind her. But she pushed on to make it the few miles into town, back to her condo.

Finally she could stand her shaking hands and ragged breathing no longer. Kenzie swerved to the shoulder and slammed the car into Park.

"God, I just…" Her voice trailed off, and she could not form words to pray. "I'm just being silly," she chided herself aloud. "God, I know that You're in control. I don't know why I'm acting like a jitterbug tonight—"

Suddenly a hand clamped over her mouth, cutting off her words and her breath.

THREE

Kenzie tried to scream, but the calloused hand covering her mouth effectively cut off all sound and stole almost all of her breath. She struggled to rip the fingers from her face, but another arm snaked around her middle, pinning her to the driver's seat, her arms at her sides.

She could not think, could not focus. She could only react, fighting with all her might against the corded arms wrapped around her.

Futilely, she tried to bite the fingers at her mouth, but only managed to nibble on a knuckle. Tossing her head from side to side, she tried to free herself, but the arms were immovable.

After what seemed an hour but was likely closer to five minutes, she was too tired to fight anymore. Sliding back against the seat, she tried another tactic. She would reason with the man sitting behind her. Craning her neck to look at him through the rearview mirror, she could barely make out the outline of rumpled hair and broad shoulders. But it was too dark for her to see any of his features.

He sat quietly, just holding her to the seat, seemingly unsure of what he wanted to do next. Finally, he whispered in her ear, "Are you done struggling?"

Her eyes flew open at his voice. She knew that voice. It was the same voice that made her stomach drop to her toes and sent shivers up and down her back.

Gasping, she garbled something unintelligible into his hand. She had trusted him, and now he was going to—well, she wasn't sure what he was going to do. But it wasn't going to be good, that was for sure.

"Shh. Calm down," he whispered into her ear. His voice was deep and soothing, and his restraints were just tight enough to hold her in place. He didn't hurt her as long as she sat still.

She made another wild attempt to free herself, trying to grab for the door handle or honk the horn. His arm around her waist suddenly squeezed, stealing all of her breath and robbing her of all her strength. He must have felt the whoosh of air expel from her lungs through her nose, because he relaxed his grip over her mouth.

Almost limp in his arms, Kenzie felt defeated. "What do you want?" she wheezed between his fingers.

"I want you to turn the car around and start driving. I want you to take me farther from the prison and to freedom. I'll tell you where to go."

Kenzie's mind worked as fast as it could under the strained circumstances. She had to get back to the prison or to a lighted, busy area. Here he was free to do with her as he pleased. It probably meant death. Or worse.

"You know who my grandfather is, don't you? If you kidnap me, there'll be no pardon. He'll hunt you down and prosecute you to the fullest extent of the law. Please think about this." She was very proud that she kept her voice from shaking with emotion and fear as she spoke.

Suddenly the arm around her middle moved and was quickly replaced by the point of a knife in her side.

"Just do what I say, Kenzie." He had never called her by her first name before, and it sparked a fire back into her.

"No. You don't want to do this. This can only end poorly for you. Think about what you're doing!"

"No arguments. Just do it. Now." His voice a growl, she knew he meant what he said.

Obeying his command, she pulled her car back onto the two-lane road, heading away from Evergreen.

A couple hundred yards away from the turnoff for the prison, she let her foot off the accelerator, hoping to swing the car down the short road to the front gate. Even if they crashed, it would be better than being alone with Myles outside the prison walls. Alone, where he could do whatever he wanted.

"Don't even think about slowing down," he commanded. He stuck the knife farther into her side, and she winced.

She yanked the wheel to the right, toward the prison road, but suddenly he was practically beside her, his long arm holding the steering wheel steady. In her frazzled state she was no match for his strength.

The lights of the prison appeared and vanished in just a moment. Protected by trees lining the road, the prison was no longer visible, and Kenzie was alone on a long stretch of road, likely leading to her death.

After all, her life was worth nothing to him now.

He despised doing this. And he hated himself for having to be in this position.

His missions usually didn't end up like this, but it still had to be done. He wasn't about to delude himself into thinking that he had a choice about kidnapping the governor's grand-daughter. He had to do this to protect her.

And even worse, he was under strict instructions from his supervisor not to reveal his true identity under any circumstances. According to Nate, if Kenzie leaked his identity to anyone else, the entire operation would be blown. The only two people in the world who knew Myles's purpose inside the prison were him and Nate. If word got out that he was investigating the trouble Kenzie was in—before all the culprits had revealed themselves—his investigation would crumble, and Nate would know exactly who spilled the beans.

Now that he'd had to kidnap her, he had no choice but to get her to a safe house. There he'd tell her who he was and what he knew of the situation. Until then, he couldn't be sure that Whitestall hadn't bugged the car. After all, he'd supplied the car key, so he'd had access to it. And what if they were stopped somewhere? Even if the kidnapping failed, he could still use the situation to smoke out the people plotting Kenzie's murder—as long as his cover remained intact. Telling her the truth right now was a risk Myles just couldn't take.

It was torture, scaring Kenzie like this. Over and over in his mind, he reminded himself that it would end soon. They just had to make one quick stop before the safe house so Myles could get in touch with Guard Whitestall. And the safest place Myles knew was a bit off the beaten path—well worth the seventy-five-mile trip out of the way.

But with every visible tremble and shudder of Kenzie's tiny form, he hated himself just a little bit more. How had it gotten to this? Who would want to harm her?

She inhaled, then let out a halted screech as her ribs came back in contact with the point of the knife. He pulled back on the blade. From his vantage point, squatting on the floor behind the driver's seat, he could see her shoulders tense again.

How was he ever going to win back her trust? That thought surprised him. Why did it suddenly matter that she trust him at all?

God, am I completely botching this? I just want to protect Kenzie, and instead, I've made her terrified and am taking her as far from civilization as I can. Show me how to solve this situation. Show me what You want, because I don't know what I'm doing here. I believe that You have a plan. Make it clear to me. I'm begging here. I'm always lost without You.

"Myles, what are you going to do with me?"

Kenzie's terse words ripped him from his silent conversation with God.

Calm her down. Soothe her fears. Speak softly.

With all the best intentions, Myles sighed. "Don't worry about it. Just keep your eyes on the road." Not exactly what he'd wanted to say, but it would have to do for now. He knew the truth. He couldn't do this assignment well while worrying about her feelings. He'd botch the job more than ever if he let his emotions seep in. Still, he could be more kind. "I'm sorry." This time his words were soft and reassuring.

"It would help if I knew what I was looking for," she said.

"You're looking for the white and yellow lines. Try to stay between them."

He could see her profile in the darkness, and she opened her mouth to speak, then quickly shut it.

He took pity on her, suddenly contrite for his sarcasm, "I'll tell you when we get closer." She nodded, but kept her lips clamped closed. And not for the first time, he took several seconds to appreciate her simple beauty and sharp personality. Someday she would make some man very lucky.

Not him, of course. He had a job to do. One that made having anyone waiting at home very difficult. Marriage and a family were years away.

Right now there was only the job. Only protecting Kenzie.

The car hit a major bump in the road, and the knife jammed into her side, snagging the silky material of her sweater.

"Would you mind moving that? I'm not going anywhere. I won't be jumping out of this car at sixty miles an hour." Her voice waivered slightly, not in fear, but like she was trying desperately not to let her anger get the better of her. She was used to giving commands. It must be killing her to be so out of control.

"As you wish." He chuckled, pocketing the little blade and thinking of that line used in his favorite childhood movie. "But don't make me regret it."

Somehow, Myles didn't think that it would matter if he had the seven-inch Bowie knife that Guard Whitestall had initially told him to take. Kenzie's response would be the same— fighting anger along with trepidation. She was a spicy spitfire if ever there was one.

No complaints, just steely determination to make it through this.

She didn't know it yet, but she *would* make it through this. He would make sure of that. He never failed to do his job.

First, Myles needed to figure out why he had been told to escape, to kidnap Kenzie and then to kill her. Whitestall had to have the answers. He would be Myles's first phone call when they arrived at their destination.

A green sign along the road read: REDMOND 73 MILES.

"Do you see that grove of trees up ahead?"

"Yes."

"Turn onto that gravel road right after them." He couldn't see the road yet, but he knew it would be there, the way it had been since his childhood.

Kenzie made a smooth turn onto the bumpy road, slowing down to accommodate the shifting gravel.

After a few minutes he said, "Make a right at that fence post."

Again Kenzie followed orders, but something in her demeanor changed. She was suddenly more alert, looking frantically about the tree-lined lane. Was she trying to memorize the route or look for an escape? Probably both. Too bad she would not find anything to help her in either pursuit. These gravel roads were as unremarkable as ever.

In the foothills of the Cascades, they were already hours from the nearest town or any help for her. She'd be much safer just staying with him.

Every second on the road took them farther and farther away from Evergreen. The tiny Oregon town had been her home for two years because of its proximity to the prison. The drive was barely ten minutes from her rented condo to the front gate of the prison, but now she drove in the opposite direction. When Mac and Nana started looking for her, they would start in Evergreen. They'd never think to look for her here.

Every moment she drove plunged her deeper and deeper into the wooded darkness. Away from the familiar. Away from safety. Away from Mac, who was likely completely unaware of her situation. She was at Myles's mercy now.

That truth shook her very core.

Send Mac. Please! Send someone to rescue me! God, I need his help right now! I think Myles is going to kill me.

Admitting that she believed she was going to die scared Kenzie beyond belief and caused her to slam on the brakes.

Myles's large body crashed into the back of her seat, sending her into the unforgiving steering wheel. He grumbled loudly. "What's wrong?"

"Everything!" she screamed. "You're going to kill me! I'm going to die, and you're making me drive to my burial ground!" She clamped her hands over her mouth, eyes wide, realizing what she had just said.

Oh, she'd been doing so well, holding herself together, searching for an opportunity to escape. But when fear and anger mixed, she could not be held responsible for what came out of her mouth. She put her face in her hands and let out a single, wild sob. Thankful that the car had stopped when she'd slammed on the brake, she dropped her forehead and rested it against the steering wheel.

Her shoulders shook, and each trembling breath required a concentrated effort not to expel a sob.

With amazing agility for such a large man, Myles squeezed between the two front seats and over the center console. Slipping into the passenger seat, he pulled her quaking form into a tight hug. His arms wrapped around her, subduing her trembles. One of his large hands cupped the top of her head and smoothed down her hair until it wrapped around the nape of her neck. He used his nimble fingers to force her to look up into his face.

The only lights came from the dashboard and the headlights pointing into nothingness. They cast a small glow inside the car, and she could see one of his eyes looking right into her face.

"Everything's going to be okay."

Even now, she found that she wanted to trust him, to look into his face and believe that he was telling her the truth. He was strong and capable. But he was also a hardened criminal, an escaped convict and her abductor.

He couldn't be trusted.

"D-don't," she stammered pushing against him. His proximity was too close, too personal, too intimate. She didn't want to be this close to someone so dangerous. Someone who made her heart beat frantically in fear. Someone who, at the same time, made her feel something very different than fear.

"Don't what?" Myles rumbled. He didn't move back even a fraction of an inch, and his breath fanned her face, invading her space all the more.

"Don't try to make me feel better after you—you—you kidnapped me!"

"Aren't you a little old to be kidnapped?" He chuckled.

"That's not the point and you know it! You got out of prison, now let me go!" Her voice rose in aggravation, but kept an even pitch. She tried to push against him again, tried to create more space between them, but he was immovable. "You're in my bubble," she finally said, her temper making her respond completely inappropriately to an armed felon.

He laughed out loud, a deep, rich sound that would have been contagious in any other situation. "Your bubble?"

"Yes, my bubble!" she said, indignation rapidly rising. "My space, my personal space. You're invading it."

"Are you trying to tell me to back off?"

"Yes!"

He laughed again as he let her go and leaned back into the passenger seat. Stretching his long legs out as much as allowed by the compact car, he propped his hands behind his head and said, "Drive on. We've got a ways to go yet tonight."

The infuriating man! She stomped on the gas pedal, sending the car bouncing into the inky night. The thick tree line on their right began to thin as they plunged headlong into the darkness.

Kenzie tried to focus on finding another road or sign of life in this wilderness. Any sign of civilization could save her.

Her eyes scanned feverishly back and forth to no avail. All she could see was the ditch on the left side of the road and sporadic pine trees on the right.

Suddenly a small deer darted through the headlights, and she slammed on the brakes for the second time that night, just missing the little creature. "Probably just running from a mountain lion," Myles mumbled, sounding half-asleep.

How could he be falling asleep? He was kidnapping her, and he was falling asleep?

She took a deep breath and pushed her indignation aside.

All the better for her if he wasn't paying attention—it meant he wouldn't notice her planning her escape.

Her focus on just that plan, she looked for intersections crossing the road. But there were none. No mailboxes along the gravel indicating a house down a driveway. No street signs. Nothing. No indication of where they were, or where they had been. Miles and miles from Evergreen or any other town.

Would Myles be caught before something terrible happened? Would they ever track and find him? Whatever his plan was, it seemed to be working. They probably didn't even know he was missing from the prison yet. And she had no plans for the evening, so no one would report her as missing until the next day. Everything seemed to be going his way. Even the fine gravel conspired to keep them from being tracked, billowing up behind the tires and then settling down over their tracks.

But Mac would find her. He always did.

A movement beside her drew her attention. Myles rubbed his left knee, kneading the muscles of his thigh directly above his kneecap, as though in pain. His eyes appeared to be closed, and a grimace wrinkled his forehead and pinched his lips. His long fingers spanned his knee and massaged the tendons on either side.

He made no other indication that he was awake.

Kenzie turned back to the road ahead, her eye catching for an instant on the green digital clock on the dashboard, reading 12:17 a.m. Had they really left the prison more than two hours before? How long ago had they left the paved road? She had no idea! She mentally kicked herself for not paying more attention to such an important detail.

"Lamebrain," she mumbled.

"You say something?" Myles asked, his voice not even husky from sleep.

"No." She sat ramrod straight, turning the car along a slight curve.

Silence reigned for several more minutes. Suddenly Myles said, "Stop here."

"Where?"

"Right here."

She slowed to a stop and peered through the windshield, searching for the reason he told her to stop.

And suddenly she saw it. A small log cabin straight ahead of them. How had he known where to stop? This entire scenario was altogether too strange. How had she gotten caught up in this? Why had Myles chosen her?

She was an easy mark. She made herself an easy mark. That's why he chose her. She had let down her guard in his presence, and he took advantage of it.

"Here we are," he announced, getting out of the car after snatching the keys from the ignition. "Let's go."

Myles took a step out of the car, and his left knee almost buckled beneath him. He stumbled, but caught himself before falling all the way to the gravel. As he swiped at the keys that he had immediately taken from Kenzie then promptly dropped, his knee screamed again.

He hated the stupid high school football injury. His dream of being a navy SEAL had crashed around him the moment his ACL snapped when the Yuma High Criminals' defensive lineman sacked him in the city championship game.

Now the doctors said that the scar tissue from the original repair surgery was inflamed and would keep him in pain until they did another surgery. But then he got this assignment. It was hard to get good medical attention in prison. It was hard to get much of anything in prison. But the mission would be over soon. They were only a hundred miles from the safe house. And he had a good feeling about Whitestall. He would wrap up this investigation quickly.

Righting himself before Kenzie even exited the car, he stalked toward the cabin's front door. His knee cooperated by sheer force of his will as he berated himself for squatting for so long.

A jumpy Kenzie slowly followed him toward the cabin, her eyes darting around the blackness. Natural beauty would soon surround them in the golden glow of the sunrise.

Now the moon cast an ethereal radiance around the young woman's tiny frame. Her usually angelic features hardened as she glared into his face. She hated him. He tried to convince himself that it didn't bother him.

"Why won't you let me go?" she tried again.

"I can't. Not yet." It was the truth. Well, mostly the truth.

Lost in thoughts of the truths he hadn't told and tugging at the water-warped cabin door that refused to open, he almost missed Kenzie's sudden spin and quick steps toward the woods on his right. His hand shot out, and he grabbed her elbow. "Not so fast."

When the door opened with a pop, he pushed her inside, following so closely that he could smell the lingering remnants of her citrus perfume. Lemon and lime.

He led her to the only seat in the room, a wooden rocking chair next to the hearth, and let go of her arm as she sank obediently between the arms, worn smooth from years of use. She looked like a child, staring at him as though he had all the answers. But he didn't. He just prayed that Whitestall had the answers they needed to save them both.

A movement in the doorway leading to the bathroom caught his eye and he turned toward the white-haired woman in the flannel nightgown walking toward him.

"Grams." He sighed, pulling the plump woman in his arms.

"Myles, what on earth are you doing here?" she asked, pulling back to look between him and Kenzie. Her brow furrowed, but she left her hands resting on his forearms. "It's the middle of the night!"

"We're—" he began, but was instantly interrupted by another voice.

"He kidnapped me! Please, you have to help me!" Kenzie charged across the room, imploring his grandma for help. Kenzie's fingers folded over each other as though almost in prayer, and she looked like she would fall on her knees at any moment.

Myles gazed into his grandma's face and spoke to her the whole truth without saying a word. His eyes beseeched her to understand the situation, to trust him. He had given her nothing to worry about for years. She could trust him.

But he also knew that Kenzie could be persuasive, and if he wasn't careful, Grams would reveal too much before he could get Kenzie to the safe house and convince her that everything he'd done, he had had to do to protect her.

Grams's eyes squinted back at him for a long moment. He squeezed her arms gently and smiled. She nodded and looked back at Kenzie.

"You're safe here, dear," she said, reaching out and taking Kenzie's hand.

Kenzie looked dumbfounded, her eyes huge in her face, her eyebrows reaching toward her hairline. "But he's kidnapped me. From the prison. He was in prison. Don't you understand?"

"You were in prison?" Grams asked, looking over her shoulder at him and quirking an eyebrow.

Myles grinned and shrugged. "It's a long story. I'll explain later."

Grams nodded and turned back to Kenzie. "I'm Lenora Borden. And you are…?"

"Kenzie—Kenzie Thorn." She tripped on her words.

"Well, welcome. You must be starving. He's *always* starving." She indicated Myles with a nod of her head. "I'll run down to the cellar and bring up some homemade beef stew. We have just a few jars left from last season's canning."

"Thanks, Grams," Myles said, giving her a peck on her cheek. "Sounds great! I'm going to make a quick phone call."

Grams nodded, then disappeared out the front door, leaving Kenzie looking so shocked that Myles pushed her gently into the rocking chair before her legs crumpled.

"Don't move," he commanded as he stalked to the telephone sitting on the kitchen counter. It was the only phone line in the house, the only way of communication. Cell phones didn't work this far out of town. And he'd never bothered to have the Internet installed. Being in touch with the outside world defeated his usual purpose for being in the cabin, and it would serve him well now. Even if Whitestall tried to trace the call, he'd have a hard time finding this place. That was what made it so perfect.

Out of the corner of his eye, he watched Kenzie settle a little deeper into the chair. A quick swipe through the pocket of his jeans produced another item the guard had given him. The tiny slip of paper contained only a single telephone number, a way of contacting the guard when the job was done.

Punching in the ten digits, Myles tapped his foot impatiently.

"Hello?" The man's voice on the other end of the line quivered slightly.

"Boss, it's Parsons."

"Parsons? Is—is everything taken care of?" For the first time in his experience with the prison guard, Myles thought he heard a bit of apprehension in the other man's voice, but Whitestall quickly subdued it.

"Almost." He shot a look in Kenzie's direction. She sat with her hands folded neatly in her lap, prim little sweater wrapped around her shoulders.

"What does that mean?" The other man whispered so softly that Myles pressed the receiver harder to his ear and focused intently on his words.

"I'm just finishing up a few things. You know. Taking care of details."

"So it's done? I mean, you killed her?"

"That is what you wanted, isn't it?"

Silence hung on the line for several long seconds. "Of course it is. I told you to take care of her. Get her out of the picture. They want her gone."

"Who's they?" Myles tried to ignore the tug of loathing he felt for the man's contempt for life in general and Kenzie specifically. Instead he focused on discovering the leader behind the contract to kidnap and murder Kenzie.

"They. Them. They...they told me to take care of it. He said if I didn't, I'd be fish food. And I believe him, but—" Whitestall's voice cut off, almost like the phone line had gone dead.

"Boss? You still there?"

"I'm here."

Myles tried to choose his words wisely. Could he draw out the other man's concerns about the plan without alerting him to the fact that he was doing so? That "but" had been a loaded one. It spelled fear. And maybe something more. "You ever think maybe you know too much? Maybe you're not safe, either."

No noise from the other end of the line. Had he pushed too hard? Finally, "Yeah, I thought of that."

"But there's nothing tying you to my escape or the murder. You'll be fine."

"Maybe. Maybe no-ot." The lilt in his voice at the end of the last word told Myles that he'd pressed too hard, frightened the guy beyond opening up. That fear was the first break in Whitestall's armor. He may be a rough and intimidating prison guard, but he was still human. And now Myles had a gut feeling he was going to run.

For his life.

Suddenly the line went dead, and the force of an unexpected blow to his left knee sent Myles crashing to the ground, howling in pain and clawing at the counter on his way down. His hands caught onto the base of the telephone and ripped the cord from the wall just as his cheek met the rough wooden floor. Tears immediately sprang to his eyes, blurring his vision of Kenzie's shoes beating a hasty getaway and the cabin door slamming behind her.

FOUR

Just follow the gravel road. Follow the road. There has to be another cabin. You'll find someone to help you.

God, please let there be someone else out here. Please send help. Send Mac.

She repeated the words over and over in her mind, never forgetting that finding help equaled freedom. Safety. Mac.

Kenzie's hands still shook violently. She'd never been in a fight before, but this was no time to back down. She had kicked Myles in the knee as hard as she could and run for all she was worth. And she was still going at full speed.

She ran between the trees lining the cleared road, but the top branches all but blocked the moonlight. She could barely see to put one foot in front of the other and couldn't see the drooping limbs that scratched at her face and arms, snagging her sweater and ripping at her cheeks and forehead. But she was afraid to run on the road. She would be far too visible to Myles if he pursued her in a car.

She ran as fast as she could manage in the uncomfortable dress shoes she'd worn to match her black skirt. A rush of thankfulness swept through her as she realized that she could be fighting the high heels she had considered wearing, even if they broke a prison rule. She had wanted to be taller than usual, to appear more intimidating with Myles in her class-room. But the uneven ground plus the heels would have equaled disaster.

Still, the impractical shoes pinched her toes with each step. The slick soles slipped along the moist earth, rolling over twigs and leaves as she raced toward freedom. Sliding over a piece of moss, she lost her balance and fell to her hands and knees.

Mud caked on her hands and skirt, and she pushed herself up. She took another deep breath and ignored the stitch in her side. The woods were silent, other than the leaves and twigs crunch-ing under her footsteps. No sounds of Myles's pursuit. But he wouldn't just let her get away. He wanted something from her, she was certain. But what? What could she possibly give him?

Her skin crawled to think.

She could not think about those things. Not right now. She had to run.

After what felt like hours, her lungs burned too badly to continue, and she lunged for a nearby tree, seeking the pro-tection of its wide trunk. Knees weak, she sagged against the rough bark.

"Oh, God, what is going on here?" she whispered.

None of it made sense, especially not Myles's grandmother, who seemed completely oblivious to her cries for help.

And then the sobs came, completely of their own volition, and she was powerless to stop them. Weak and ashamed of her weakness, she let herself cry, all the while keeping a lis-tening ear for the sounds of footsteps behind her.

Her own arms wrapped tightly around her middle against the icy, early morning air, and with her head leaning back against the tree trunk, she could almost fall asleep from the sheer physical and mental exhaustion of the last several hours.

Almost.

Suddenly feather-light footfalls to Kenzie's left caught her attention. Holding her breath, she waited to see what approached. Expecting a wild bear, or worse—Myles Parsons—she laughed out loud as a deer darted in front of her, stopped and sniffed the air. The creature took a second whiff and bounded off.

Relieved it was only a harmless doe, Kenzie began picking her way through the brush once again. Follow the road. Just follow the road and find another cabin. She could hardly wait for the sun to make its first appearance over the horizon and provide a touch of warmth to the frigid air.

Suddenly a memory halted her in her tracks. In the car Myles had said something about deer. Was that one running from a mountain lion?

A rustling of leaves and brush produced her answer almost immediately as yellow eyes glowed eerily to her left. The answer was a resounding *yes*.

"Oh, God!" It was the only prayer she could offer before covering her eyes and backing up against the nearest tree.

"That girl!" Myles snarled as his knee buckled beneath his weight yet again. Had she no sense of self-preservation? They were in the mountains—the weather was liable to change at any moment. And what about the wild animals out and about? The sun was hours away from its first appearance, so all of the nightly predators still roamed the area. She'd put herself in serious danger by running off like that—and leaving him in so much pain that he almost couldn't go after her.

But he'd promised himself he'd protect her. Because it was his job, of course. So he'd scraped himself off the floor and followed her trail.

Of course Kenzie had kicked his injured knee. She must have seen him rubbing it in the car. He had to remember that she was both smarter and spicier than he originally gave her credit for.

He grumbled under his breath at the tree branch that nicked his face as he hobbled along the trail Kenzie left. "God, I'm a little angry here," he prayed in a tense whisper. "Could You please help me to calm down so I can find Kenzie and get her back to safety?"

The breeze chilled him as he took a deep breath. Leaves rustled as small animals scurried away from night predators. He wondered where that tiny deer they had seen on the drive to the cabin was hiding. Was it still being chased by a mountain lion? Or had the mountain lion found new prey?

As angry as he was, that question spurred him to a faster speed. He had to hurry. Kenzie had already been on the run far too long. It was dangerous out here. Once he got her to safety, he would explain as much as he could. If Nate chewed him out for it later, so be it.

When he finally heard Kenzie's stick-snapping footsteps, he knew that he was not far behind. Picking up his pace, he whizzed by a deer. It took a split second for the animal's meaning to fully sink into his distracted mind.

Deer. Mountain lion.

Crud!

Myles growled to himself as he picked up his pace, sneaking up to the small clearing ahead of him. In the darkness, he began to make out the purple of Kenzie's sweater and the red curls of her hair. Her hands covered her face as she stood stock-still against the trunk of a tree.

Opposite a large female mountain lion.

The woman had no sense of self-preservation. And wasn't it just his rotten luck that he was committed to keeping her around?

That meant he was going to have to take some sort of action.

God, protect me and this crazy woman!

Without a second thought or prayer, he jumped in front of

Kenzie's shaking form, between her and the snarling cat crouched a few feet away.

"What are you doing?" she whispered into his ear, clinging to his shoulders.

Was she serious? He was saving her tail, whether or not she realized or liked it, and she picked that moment to start up a conversation?

"Shush," he whispered, barely audibly.

The striped cougar hunched a little lower then bared its long, yellow teeth.

"Is it going to attack?" she asked, her voice shaking with fear.

"What do you think?"

He could feel her head nodding into his right shoulder, her tiny fingers digging sharply into his shoulder blade and deltoid. Thankful for small miracles, he noted that she kept her fingernails short.

"Why are you protecting me?"

Myles sighed heavily. This was hardly the ideal moment for this conversation. But if something happened to him, she had a right to know she would still be in danger. And at least he could be certain that these woods weren't bugged, unlike the car. "I'm an FBI agent. I was assigned to protect you inside the prison."

"What?" Her whisper spoke volumes of disbelief.

"I'll explain the details later." Suddenly the cat shifted and growled deep in the back of its throat.

"If we're silent, will it leave us alone?"

"I don't know. We're not being very silent, are we?" He did his best to keep his voice low, but it barely mattered. Of course the cat was going to attack. With one eye on the animal and one glancing into her face over his shoulder, he tried to offer a reassuring smile.

She clamped both hands over her mouth, her eyes huge in

the strained planes of her face as she realized that she was still talking.

Myles almost laughed out loud. If he had been anywhere else in the world, he would have let out a great belly laugh at the look of panic and shock on Kenzie's face. But this was not the time or place to ponder that expression. There would be time enough for that later, if they survived.

Yellow eyes glowed in the moonlight as the fur on the mountain lion's back began to stand up. Completely unprepared, Myles was about to fight a mountain lion to protect Kenzie Thorn. When had he gone insane?

Suddenly he wished for the knife that Guard Whitestall had offered him back at the prison. But wishes don't scare off mean, angry cougars.

Kenzie gasped, squeezing him even tighter, and Myles knew it was time. This was it. Either God was going to spare his life, or he was going to meet his Maker.

The cat lunged, teeth bared, claws spread wide, as it jumped toward his throat. He dodged left, simultaneously pushing Kenzie behind the tree, out of the path of the mountain lion. A searing pain shot through his right thigh as the force of the seventy-five-pound animal knocked him to the ground.

On the ground, he lost most of the momentum of a blow, but with as much force as he could muster, he punched the animal in the tender flesh of its nose. The cat whined, then immediately growled, whipping its head from side to side.

It was enough time for Myles to jump back up to his feet, digging in his pocket for the pocket knife that had snagged Kenzie's sweater earlier in the night. He flicked it open as fast as he could and jabbed it into the cat's cheek as it jumped at him again. The force of the animal's momentum and Myles's swinging arm shoved the knife completely into the tender flesh.

Stunned and wounded, the cat dropped to the ground,

trying to dislodge the offending object. It backed away slowly, head still swinging from side to side. Then it turned and bolted.

Head spinning and physically drained, Myles dropped to his knees and fell forward on his face. He could barely make out the horrified expression on Kenzie's face before everything went black.

Kenzie threw herself onto the ground next to Myles's lifeless form. She couldn't tell if he was breathing, and blood pooled around the jagged gash in his thigh. She had to do something.

Kneeling next to the body, wringing her hands, she thought about her options. Oh, she considered leaving him to fend for himself, if he wasn't dead already. After all, he was probably just out to kill or hurt her anyway. What he said about being an FBI agent was a lie anyway. Wasn't it?

She could make a run for it. Find safety and get back to her family.

But if Myles was going to hurt her, then why did he save her from the mountain lion? Why put himself in such danger? Why offer such a far-fetched lie about who he was?

She heaved a loud sigh, knowing that she couldn't possibly leave him there. She reached out and gently touched his neck, feeling for a pulse. It was thready and weak. She didn't have much time. But there was no possible way she could carry him back to the cabin.

"God, I need some help here!" she cried out to the still air, trying to remember what she'd learned in the first-aid class they'd made her take at the prison.

Suddenly she remembered. Stop or slow the flow of blood from the wound. She whipped off her cardigan sweater and tied it around his leg, just above the bleeding wound. The beautiful purple sweater immediately began turning crimson, but the blood pool on the ground stopped spreading.

"Now, how to get him back to the cabin?" She rubbed her head, sizing up his tall frame and broad shoulders. She could not carry him back to the cabin. It had to be at least three miles back.

Just then moonlight glinted off a silver object poking out the pocket of his jeans. Where had he gotten jeans and a T-shirt? Why hadn't she noticed before that he wasn't wearing his orange prison jumpsuit?

There wasn't time to analyze his clothes, so she snatched the key out of his pocket and sprinted the same way she had come. She ignored her ragged breathing and sharp pain in her chest, reaching the cabin in what seemed a split second.

"Lenora! Lenora!" she yelled between gasped breaths. "It's Myles! He's been hurt!"

Lenora's round frame appeared in the doorway in seconds. Outfitted in her flannel shirt, sweat pants and slippers, she sailed toward Kenzie, grabbing her shoulders and shaking her just enough to pull her into reality. "What's happened? Where's Myles?"

"He— There was a mountain lion. It was going to attack me, and he saved me!" Tears of frustration and overwhelming emotion poured down her cheeks. "He's hurt," she hiccupped. "Please help me!"

Lenora nodded and grabbed the keys from her hand, sliding behind the wheel of the car as Kenzie dove into the passenger seat. The tires kicked up dirt and gravel as she floored the gas pedal in the direction that Kenzie indicated.

When they arrived at the scene of the attack five minutes later, Lenora pulled the car as close to the still form on the ground as possible, dodging two tall pine trees.

Kenzie raced around the car and whipped the back door open as Lenora ran to her injured grandson. Then, mustering all their strength, the two women grabbed Myles's arms and dragged him to the car. Grunting and shoving, they managed to jostle him into the backseat. When his leg landed on the ancient upholstery, a crimson pool grew where it lay.

The car couldn't reach the cabin fast enough.

When Lenora finally skidded to a halt, she and Kenzie again dragged Myles's lifeless body toward the front door. The door was slightly ajar, so Kenzie kicked it all the way open as they tugged Myles up the two steps and through the door.

Kenzie sucked in uneven breaths and leaned on her knees when he was finally deposited on the bed. Lenora sat on the edge of the wooden bed frame, leaning over Myles's wan face.

How had they been able to do that? If Kenzie thought about the impossibility of the task, she could not believe two women had actually gotten such a large man all the way back to the cabin and onto the bed.

Right now, there was time only to think about getting things done. Myles's wounds needed to be cleaned and bandaged. Determined to try to save his life, as he had done for her, she rolled up her sleeves and set to the task of helping Lenora patch him up.

FIVE

Kenzie sighed loudly, wiping her forehead with the back of her arm. She kept her hands, red and sticky with blood, away from her face. Myles lay motionless on the bed. He had only once regained consciousness for a few seconds while she and Lenora cleaned and dressed the seven-inch gash just above his right knee.

Now sleep called her, as well, refusing to let her fight. Her body ached from sheer exhaustion as she stumbled to the sink in the small cabin's kitchen and rinsed her hands. She barely made it to the wooden rocking chair before her eyes closed of their own accord. She felt Lenora lay a thick quilt over her just before she succumbed to the exhaustion that beckoned.

Her rest was fitful, filled with images of Myles, memories of the touch of his hand in her classroom. His protection and rescue. Over and over her dreams played the scene as Myles jumped in front of her. The mountain lion's bared fangs. Its attack. Myles's lifeless form on the ground.

"Ahh!" she screamed, waking herself up.

Sweat dripping from her temples, she shuddered violently, effectively waking herself up completely. Her digital watch read 2:30 p.m. The afternoon sun streamed through the only window. She took a long look around the single room, taking in the rough wooden walls, large empty fireplace and door that led to the miniature bathroom.

"Good afternoon," Lenora greeted her softly. "Why don't you get cleaned up, and I'll make us some eggs for lunch?" Her smile was kind and Kenzie wished she had properly thanked her the night before.

Standing on shaky legs, she staggered toward the bathroom, then leaned against the door. "God, please, let there be soap," she mumbled.

In the cracked, clouded mirror above the sink, she barely recognized the face staring back at her. She ran her fingers through her auburn hair, making it as presentable as possible. Never mind that there was no one to make it presentable for. Lenora and Myles could not possibly care less about her appearance. The angry red scratches on her cheeks and neck looked worse than they felt. And they definitely did not feel good.

She poked at an especially jagged red line that ran from the corner of her mouth to her jaw line. Pressing her tongue into that part of her lower lip, she angled for a better look. A red smear pooled below it on her neck, but it didn't seem to need stitches. Even if it did, there would be no acquiring them. Not here.

Her face tender and her whole body aching, she gingerly bent to look for soap in the rough wooden cabinets beneath the sink.

Score!

Snatching the little bar of blue soap, she ran it beneath a steady stream of only slightly brown water pouring from the faucet. At least it was warm. And the soap worked up a good lather as she scrubbed under her fingernails. Then she gently rubbed her cheeks, forehead and neck.

When she looked into the mirror five minutes later, she recognized the face shining back. And for the first time in almost twenty-four hours, the face smiled back at her, just so grateful to feel safe and clean.

"It's good to be human again," she said to the mirror.

As she walked back into the main room, her stomach growled loudly. "That was almost loud enough to wake Myles, I bet." And then she did something she hadn't done in more than a day. She giggled. It felt good to use those facial muscles again, to feel her lips twitch and return to old habits.

She had almost forgotten that Lenora was even there, so her husky chuckle made Kenzie jump. "You must be starving. With all the excitement last night," Lenora seemed to say to herself, "we didn't even get to eat the beef stew I brought up. Oh, well. It'll make a good dinner." She smiled again as Kenzie's stomach let out another grumble.

Embarrassed, Kenzie wrapped her arms around her middle. She tried to return the older woman's smile, but suddenly felt self-conscious.

From her place by the little kitchen stove, Lenora asked, "Did you sleep well?"

"Um…yes, fine, thanks." Briefly scanning the room, she saw a few blankets spread on the floor next to the bed where Myles lay, and she realized what Lenora had sacrificed. "Did you sleep on the floor? I'm so sorry. I didn't even think!"

"Don't concern yourself about it. I've slept on the floor many times. When my boys were young and we would come here to hunt, I often slept on the floor. It wasn't until my boys had boys of their own that they realized that I deserved the bed." She chuckled to herself, apparently lost in fond memories.

"Do you—do you live here?" Kenzie stumbled on the question, shuddering at even the thought of living so far from Evergreen all alone, so deep in the forest. She couldn't remember passing any towns on the road the night before.

Lenora laughed. "Oh, heavens no!" Her hand stirred a skillet of scrambled eggs with a skilled hand as she glanced over her shoulder at Kenzie. "I live in a Jack's Hollow about a forty-five-minute drive away—the opposite direction from Evergreen. Myles asked me to check on his cabin a few times. Run the water a bit so it doesn't get brown. That kind of thing. Said he was going to be out of town—I suppose he meant in prison." She shook her head and laughed again. "That boy gets into the strangest situations. But he's a good man."

Kenzie's mind reeled. How on earth could a grandmother call prison a strange situation? Myles was a convicted felon. Who had kidnapped her. How could Lenora be so oblivious to reality? Unless Myles had told the truth about being an FBI agent. But that simply wasn't possible. Was it?

No. It couldn't be.

She opened her mouth to speak the thoughts screaming in her head, but Lenora spoke first. "I'm going to run outside and get some more firewood. We're running low, so I'm going to have to hunt for some. I'll be back in a while. Why don't you check on Myles? Then go ahead and dish up some eggs for yourself. You look like a sturdy wind would blow you over."

Kenzie only managed a nod before Lenora hustled out the door. Her stomach, still growling, told her it was time to eat. But food would have to wait.

This could be her only chance to escape. And she had to take it.

Her keys sat next to the destroyed telephone—the only phone she'd seen in the cabin. The one that Myles had broken when he crashed to the ground after she kicked his knee. She hadn't meant to eliminate a possible rescue opportunity. But how was she to know that he would land on the receiver, smashing it into five very unusable pieces?

Grabbing for the car keys that she'd thrown on the counter the night before, Kenzie dashed out the front door. The bright sun made her eyes burn as she glanced around the little clearing. It looked so much more menacing in the black of night. But the sunlight gave it a serenity that Kenzie had never felt in any other place.

She was tempted to turn around and go back into the house. Myles couldn't hurt her now, not in his current condition, and maybe she could get her questions answered. But injured or not, Myles could still be dangerous. And there was obviously something not right with Lenora. How could she not respond to an abducted woman begging for help?

"He's a terrible man. I know he is," she told herself. But somewhere in the pit of her stomach she questioned her own statement. How could such a dreadful man put himself in the path of a mountain lion to save her?

Shaking off the questions that bombarded her mind, Kenzie hurried to her car. She shot a glance at the corner of the cabin. Lenora was still around back. No time like the present to hit the road. Kenzie slipped behind the wheel of her car, shoved the key into the ignition and turned it.

Click.

She tried again and again. Same response from her car. None.

"No," she huffed to her dashboard, blowing at an annoying strand of hair falling into her face. She had to get back to Mac, to safety. How could her car not be working?

"God, I just want to go home. To get back to Mac and Nana. Please send Mac for me."

The passenger-side window was cracked open just enough that Kenzie could hear Lenora breaking twigs and crunching leaves as she walked around the house. It was hard to tell if the woman was dangerous or maybe just senile. Not sure of how the old woman would react to Kenzie's failed escape plan, Kenzie briefly considered making another run for it. But one hurried step told her she wouldn't be able to make it far. Every ounce of her ached, so she put aside that thought and hobbled back toward the house, spinning around the main room, looking for something to do to appear busy and resigning herself to staying there until Mac arrived for her.

The tiny first-aid kit Lenora had found in a kitchen cabinet the night before caught her eye. It had been less than adequate for mending Myles's wounds, but if she used it, maybe Lenora wouldn't suspect her ill-fated escape attempt. She couldn't be sure how much leeway Lenora or Myles would give her. Maybe they were both a little crazy.

Or worse, they could both be telling the truth. If Myles really was an FBI agent, she couldn't leave. She couldn't leave without knowing.

And if he really had kidnapped her in order to protect her, then she couldn't very well let him bleed to death or end up with an infection in the wound he got saving her.

She closed her eyes as she perched on the edge of the bed, and slowly tried to think through everything she knew to this point. Myles had kidnapped her, but he hadn't hurt her. When he subdued her in the car, his grip was firm, but not damaging. That toy knife he'd had had done little but snag her sweater. Somehow he'd managed to get into her car. Where had she gotten the key? And then there was Lenora. A man who so obviously loved his grandmother couldn't be all bad.

And of course there was Myles, getting in front of her and fighting a mountain lion to protect her. It just couldn't be ignored.

But did that equal to Myles being an FBI agent?

That was a question more easily asked than answered.

For now it would have to remain unanswered. The gauze covering Myles's wound was turning a very deep shade of pink. At the very least, he deserved some care, so she got back to the task at hand.

The first-aid kit was pretty sparse. A couple strips of gauze, medical scissors, which Kenzie only once considered using as a weapon to escape the night before, hydrogen peroxide that apparently burned when she poured it onto his wound—if his delirious screams were to be believed. A few alcohol pads. Sorely lacking, but all that they had to work with.

Kenzie gently lifted the gauze wrapping on his leg. Blood oozed as the gauze stuck to the crust around the gash. Her stomach lurched at the sight. Had she cleaned it well enough the night before?

Unsure, she dabbed at it with another alcohol pad.

Myles moaned loudly, and she snatched her hand away from him so fast that she nearly fell off the bed. After a moment, his breathing returned to normal, his shoulders rising and falling in a steady rhythm, and the wrinkle between his eyes smoothed.

When she finished cleaning and redressing the wound, she immediately went to the kitchen in search of plates and silverware, finally ready to soothe the growling monster in her stomach. Searching the cabinets wouldn't take long, as there were only four of them.

She gave a little squeak of surprise when the first cabinet held a large, unhappy spider. If spiders hiss, this one certainly hissed at her. She could not be 100 percent certain where its eyes were, but it seemed to glare into her face, twitching one leg at a time as if waiting to pounce on her.

Grabbing one of two books in the cabinet, she reached back to take a swing at the spider, but suddenly noticed the soft leather binding with beautiful golden-edged pages. The edges were worn and the front cover curled up slightly, as though it was thoroughly used. And there on the front cover above the embossed name *Myles Joshua Borden* were the words *Holy Bible*.

Gently setting the book on the counter, she picked up the other book, what appeared to be an old journal, and swiped at the offending bug. She smashed the spider once. Then again for good measure.

Lord, thank You for leaving something handy for me to use—something other than Your Word—to kill the spider. She picked up the Bible and hugged it to her pounding heart, her eyes glued to the crumpled mass of tangled legs on the bottom shelf of the cabinet. After a quick poke with her pinky, she confirmed that the spider was indeed deceased. Then her mind wandered to the precious book in her hands.

"What are you doing with a Bible?" Kenzie asked the sleeping figure behind her with barely a glance over her right shoulder.

"Same thing most people do with a Bible."

The sudden hammering of her heart had nothing to do with the gravelly quality of Myles's voice. "You scared me!" she stormed, marching toward his bed.

Holding up his hands in surrender, as if to ward off her attack in his sprawled position, Myles choked back what sounded suspiciously like laughter. "Not my fault. You asked me a question. It would be rude not to answer."

"Well, you should have told me you were awake! I…I… I would have…"

"You would have what, Ms. Thorn?"

She opened her mouth to respond, then snapped it closed when nothing came to mind.

"You would have offered to dish me up some of Grams's eggs?" On cue, his stomach growled almost as loudly as hers had a few minutes before. "That would be fantastic."

"I should let you starve," she grumbled, her eyebrows pulling into her most serious face, the one she used on misbehaving inmates. But before she let him slip in another retort, she spun on her toe and stalked the ten feet back into the kitchen.

It was then that she realized that she still held Myles

Borden's Bible to her chest. Setting it gently on the counter, she began moving through the cupboards, looking for anything that would serve as a plate or bowl.

After opening all four cabinets, she finally located two tin plates covered with dust. She quickly rinsed and dried them with the single dish towel hanging over the oven handle. She dished up a serving of eggs for each of them, then turned back toward Myles.

Myles's piercing blue eyes focused on her from across the room as she moved toward him. He looked relaxed, leaning on the pillow against the headboard, covered with a ratty blanket to keep the chill away. She handed him a plate, and he immediately began shoveling the fluffy, dill-flavored eggs into his mouth.

When the silence grew too heavy, Kenzie asked, "So what *is* someone like you doing with a Bible? And who's Myles Borden?"

"Someone like me?"

She felt her cheeks burn. Mac would be appalled at her choice of words. She hated disappointing him, even when he wasn't there, even if the phrase was warranted by Myles's behavior over the last twenty-four hours.

But the laughter in Myles's eyes sapped her of any embarrassment, igniting her ire instead.

"Yes. Someone like you. You know. A kidnapper and felon."

A new emotion flickered across his face—could it be shame? Regret? Fear?—but his tone was light when he said, "Like I said before. I do the same as a lot of others. I read it. I study it."

"Oh." Suddenly at a loss for words, she quickly took another bite of her breakfast. "Sorry I used your book to smash a spider."

He laughed out loud. Suddenly a coughing fit seized him

as tears rolled down his cheeks. Gasping for breath, he laughed again, "If it makes you feel any better, that's not my journal or my Bible, and I think that my grandpa would be proud to have his journal used in the noble elimination of his sworn enemy."

At Myles's use of the overly dramatic phrase, Kenzie couldn't hold back a small chuckle of her own. "Happy to help."

Nothing made much sense at this point. Myles appeared less and less like any inmate she'd ever met. But the FBI thing seemed too far-fetched. A gentle tug on her heart forced her to evaluate her doubts. If he could just prove himself to be her protector—did she need more proof than his saving her from the mountain lion?—then he could help her get back to Mac. Get back to safety.

When his grandma's famous dill pickle eggs reached his empty stomach, Myles sighed contentedly. The ache from not eating for more than a day slowly eased, as he shoved bite after bite into his mouth as fast has his semirecumbent position allowed. His swollen, throbbing leg would not permit him to sit up completely, and leaning on his left elbow left him in an awkward position.

He and Kenzie ate in relative silence; the only sounds filling the cabin were those of spoons clanking on the edge of tin camping plates. Every now and then he could hear Grams outside the cabin, making trips from the shed in the back to the front door, piling firewood.

He and Kenzie both finished their meals in record time, and she immediately grabbed the single dish from his hand and scurried over to the kitchen sink. She stood at the sink with her back to him, giving him free rein to make sure she had not been injured by the mountain lion when he collapsed.

Her slender figure seemed unharmed, save for the bright

red marks on her cheeks and neck from the tree branches. His complexion likely showed similar signs. The purple sweater that had looked so pristine in her classroom was now ruined, and her black skirt looked matted with what must be blood.

His blood.

Thank You, God, that I was the one injured and not—

"Why is your grandfather's Bible in this cabin?"

Her question interrupted his thoughts. But it was a welcome intrusion. If she was talking to him about trivial things, then she might be warming up to him. Even if she kept her back turned.

"This was his cabin. He passed it down to my father, who gave it to me a few years ago. The Bible stays with the cabin, so that when I come here to get away from it all, I always have it handy."

"What nefarious acts are you trying to get away from? Crime a little too taxing these days?" Suddenly her shoulders stiffened and she clamped both of her hands over her mouth, a becoming pink blush creeping up the back of her neck. She peeked over her shoulder and for a moment looked like a kid caught with her hand in the cookie jar.

If he hadn't been confined to the bed, he might have been tempted to pull her into a hug and kiss the top of her head like he had done the first time his cousin's four-year-old daughter pulled the cookie jar stunt.

Of course that would be completely unprofessional. Something he'd never do. He didn't really want to do it anyway. She was just an assignment.

"I'm sorry. That was rude." Her voice shook slightly, evidently repentant.

Always…well, usually…the sweet lady. "It's okay. Like I told you before, I wasn't in prison because of any 'nefarious acts.' I was there to protect you."

"But then why were you in the GED class?"

He cracked a smile. "Where else in the prison could I go to get so close to you?"

"Oh." She seemed to hold back more questions and turned to wipe the dishes.

If he could say one thing for her, she was industrious. She had had no problem serving them a meal, and she easily located the dishes and cleaned them. Judging from the bandage on his leg, she and Grams had found the first-aid kit without a problem. Although a black smudge marred her jawbone—certainly a souvenir of a face wash based on a clouded reflection in the bathroom mirror—the rest of her face looked clean.

The only real wonder was that she had yet to discover the clothing in the three-drawer, roughly hewn dresser beside the bed, and the cash stashed in the Bible. Oh, and the fact that at his request, Grams had disconnected her car battery the night before. He guessed she had done it sometime after they had brought him back to the cabin and Kenzie fell asleep. He couldn't have her running off before he got her to safety.

"I think there are some clothes that might fit you in the drawer over here. Did you not see them?"

"I saw them. I thought they might be your wife's things."

"Wife?" If he had been drinking water, it would have sprayed all over his bed.

"I saw the wedding bands, too."

Heaving a deep breath, Myles said, "Not mine."

"No?" she stole another glance at him over her shoulder. "But you said this was your cabin."

"It is, but the rings aren't mine. Definitely not. Grams's and Grandpa's. When he died about a year ago, my dad gave me his ring, and Grams gave me hers. She said she'd like to see me give it to a lady someday. It always just felt like this was the place to keep them."

After a long pause, "And the clothes?"

"Grams."

She paused a moment, as if searching for something to say. "Oh."

"Grams's things may be a little big on you, and she doesn't wash the ones she leaves here very often, but I'm sure they're better than what you have on."

She looked down at her tattered attire and nodded in acceptance. "Thanks. I think I'll try them."

Myles tried to stifle a jaw-cracking yawn as Kenzie disappeared into the bathroom, her arms loaded with jeans and flannel shirts that belonged to the most important woman in his life. Could it be a coincidence, then, that Kenzie would be wearing them now?

Eyes drooping heavily, he almost fell asleep before Kenzie's return. When she did walk through the doorway, he laughed out loud. The long-sleeve, plaid flannel shirt swallowed her whole. Briskly rolling up the sleeves that completely covered her hands and tying the hem at her narrow waist, she made the outfit look almost attractive. He'd never been an advocate of women in flannel.

Until today.

Another loud yawn caught him off guard, and he sighed loudly.

"Are you okay?" Immediately she sat on the edge of his bed, gently resting her hand against his forehead. "You don't have a fever, thankfully. Maybe it won't get infected."

Eyes still drooping shut, he managed to mumble, "Thanks for getting me back here and fixing me up."

"I couldn't just leave you out there after what you said… about the FBI…and after what you did…after you…" The silence seemed to grow as she swallowed thickly. Her gray eyes glistened, reflecting the light from the window.

Another yawn as he reached to pat her arm. "I'm so tired."

"You lost a lot of blood."

"Mmm-hmm."

She swallowed audibly again. "I know you're not really in the FBI, but…but—" Her eyes pleaded with him to prove her wrong, to reveal himself completely as her protector. But then she swallowed and tried a different tactic. "You saved my life. Why?"

He couldn't hold back the smile that tugged at the corner of his lips even as sleep beckoned to him. "We're safe here for now. If I wanted you dead, I'd have let you walk back into that prison."

SIX

What could he possibly mean? He fell into a deep sleep before she could ask him. He needed the rest, but she needed answers.

If I wanted you dead, I'd have let you walk back into that prison.

Pacing from wall to wall, ragged wooden beam to wooden beam, she marched as though she would never stop. Her mind's eye lurched from scene to scene. From seeing Myles's shape in her rearview mirror to the black night illuminated only by the headlights of the car she drove, from the feel of the knife stabbing her side to his face inches from hers, invading her personal space. From the terror of the midnight forest to Myles's bloody, broken body lying limp on the ground.

They were pieces of a puzzle.

But they didn't fit together. None of it made sense. Why would he kidnap her only to save her life? And what could he possibly mean by saying she would die if she went back into the prison? Could the FBI really be the answer?

She couldn't wait any longer! She had to know the truth. She needed proof.

Stomping over to Myles's bed, she looked down into his face and shook his sleeping shoulder. "Myles. Myles, wake up. I need to talk to you."

He grunted, still half-asleep, then opened one eye and squinted it at her. As soon as he focused on her face, both of his eyes popped open, and he was instantly awake. "What's wrong? Is someone else here? Where's Grams?"

Kenzie's hand flipped a lock of hair over her shoulder. "She brought in more wood for the fire hours ago. You were still sleeping, so she took her car to get some groceries and more bandages for your leg. She should be back soon. But don't change the subject. Tell me what's going on!"

Myles's voice was quiet but firm. "Kenzie, you know everything that I do. Like I told you, I'm FBI. Someone at the prison wanted you dead. I was put there to protect you."

Her eyes darted around the room, seeking a resting place other than his sincere gaze back at her. "I know, I know. But I need proof." This was too hard to believe without actual evidence. In her heart she knew she was a Doubting Thomas, but hadn't Christ compassionately offered proof to Thomas when he needed it most? She hoped Myles could drum up some compassion for her in her disbelief.

"What kind of proof do you want?" His eyes softened slightly.

"Something to prove you're really in the FBI. Don't you have a badge somewhere?"

He smiled and then shrugged. "Sure I do. It's in the bureau office safe in Portland. I knew I'd be stripped of everything I took into the prison, and that my belongings would be searched, so I took nothing with me." He shrugged again, and Kenzie could practically see him thinking. Finally the light bulb went on. With his chin, he pointed to the dresser. "In the bottom drawer. Under the clothes."

She fumbled through the clothes, not sure what she should be looking for. Finally her hands landed on a piece of wood, and she yanked it free, revealing a golden trophy. Her eyebrows slowly arched up as she read the inscription on the trophy.

"Everyone in my office won one of those last year when the Portland office beat all the other FBI offices in the Northwest in the annual physical fitness competition."

He wasn't lying. It was spelled out right on the trophy's inscription. "FBI Special Agent Myles Borden," she read aloud. "Borden? But your name is Myles Parsons."

"I couldn't keep my real name while I was undercover, could I?"

"So you're Myles Borden?"

"Yes."

Her mind flashed to the Bible she'd held earlier that day. "As in Myles Joshua Borden?"

"As in Myles Justin Borden. I'm named after my two grandfathers. The other Myles Borden was my dad's dad."

She sounded completely dimwitted, and she knew it. "But—but don't you have to have a law degree to be a special agent? You said you didn't even have a GED!"

"Well, technically, I don't have a GED." He grimaced as he adjusted his knee. "I told you I got into the GED class because that's where you were."

There it was. She held all the proof she needed in her hands, regardless of how far-fetched it might be. She had to believe him now.

"Why didn't you tell me before? In the car? At the prison?"

"I tried to tell you this morning in the woods. Before the mountain lion attack. You just wouldn't believe me. And before that I was on strict orders not to tell you anything. Plus, I couldn't trust that your car wasn't bugged. You see, two weeks ago our field office received a tip from a friend of Special Agent in Charge Nate Andersen that you might be in danger. There was no way of verifying it, but Andersen is a strong believer in gut instincts. He felt there might be some merit to the tip, and he trusted the instincts of the tipster, so he assigned me to enter the prison, get assigned to your GED classes, keep an eye on you and find out what was going on.

"I made nice with the superintendent, and from there it was all pretty easy. The guards seemed to leave me alone, and I earned a reputation in the yard as someone not to mess with."

"So, if you were all buddy-buddy with everyone, where did you get the—uh—black eye?" She gingerly touched the sensitive skin below her right eye.

He shrugged. "It's a hazard of the job."

"But wait, why didn't you just tell me? Why didn't Mac tell me!"

"We couldn't afford the risk of tipping off the wrong people that the bureau is involved. No one knows. Not Mac, not the superintendent. No one."

"Then why did you kidnap me?"

"I was told to."

Her mouth dropped open as she tried to put the pieces of the puzzle together, her eyes slowly shifting from left to right and back again. "By whom?"

"Guard Whitestall waylaid me on my way to class yesterday. He gave me these clothes, a knife and a key to your car." Myles produced the tiny silver object from his pocket and held it out to her. "He told me that I had to decide then and there if I was going to help him or not. If I didn't, I'm sure that we both would be in serious danger. When I told him I would help him, Whitestall told me to sneak into your car and kidnap you. Then, when we got to a remote enough location, I was to take you out of the picture."

"Take me out of the picture?" Her voice cracked, but she quickly pulled herself together, blood boiling in her veins. "He wanted you to kill me?"

"Yes."

Mac always said that JB and his guards were tough. They had to be to work in the prisons. But Kenzie thought it likely that JB was more sinister than tough, and maybe Larry was, too. There was always a glint in JB's eye that gave her goose bumps—that she took to mean *Don't test me.* So she'd steered clear of him as much as possible in her two years at the prison. But now, memories flitted back to her. Scenes of JB and Larry in their element, intimidating inmates.

The frightened face of one of her students came to mind. She recalled a time that she entered her classroom to find the man sitting at his desk, surrounded by Superintendent Ryker, Larry and another guard she didn't recognize.

"If you don't do it, we'll find someone else who will," JB had seethed through clenched teeth.

Larry petted his enormous flashlight lovingly, and the other guard glared hard at the single inmate.

A smirk tweaked Larry's less-than-handsome facial features, turning him into a frightening force. "You'll be better off doing what the superintendent says. Think about your wife, Joe. And that pretty little girl of yours. Wouldn't you like to see them again?"

The inmate launched out of his chair at the mention of his family, but the large hands of JB and the other guard helped him roughly back into his chair.

"You have twenty-four hours to make up your mind," Larry said. "Choose wisely."

With that thinly veiled threat, JB and the two guards spun and walked toward the door, where Kenzie stood rooted to the ground. "Good day, Ms. Thorn," Larry mumbled, as he took his position by the classroom door. If they had been surprised by her presence in the room, none of the three men showed it.

Now Kenzie put her face into her palms, shaking her head. Why hadn't she seen it sooner? Why didn't she investigate JB and Larry's actions toward her students? Why hadn't she considered that she might be in danger because of them?

"But why kidnap me, when you had to know that Mac would hunt you? Why didn't you just turn Larry in to the authorities and take me back to my family?"

"There's something that runs a lot deeper here than just Whitestall wanting to have you taken care of. Part of my assignment is figuring out what that is and then fixing it. But my first priority is protecting you."

"Oh, so that's why you let the mountain lion attack you." *Why did I let that pop out?* she chastised herself. Did she really want there to be another reason he would save her?

"Well, I don't usually just sit around waiting to be prey for mountain lions," Myles said, trying to lighten the mood. It suddenly felt too serious, and his throbbing leg was hurting enough that he needed something else to focus on, to smile about.

"Right." She nodded, then turned her back on him.

Did she want him to admit that he would have protected her no matter what his assignment? Well, she wasn't going to squeeze that out of him, no matter how sweet her smile or how soft her hand against his forehead. He had no intention of admitting that to himself, either.

"Something has that guard seriously spooked. I need to figure out what—or rather, who—that is. So tomorrow I'll take you the safe house. You'll be... Well, you'll be safe there." He sounded anything but articulate. This woman made him lose his ability to speak.

"No."

"No, what? I'm taking you to the safe house tomorrow.

This isn't a negotiation. I'm not taking you back to your family until we figure out what's going on."

"I'm not going to the safe house." She was definitely in spicy mode.

Rats!

"And what do you propose you'll do?" He would humor her before putting her in her place.

"I'm going with you."

SEVEN

"No, you're not." Myles's voice brooked no argument.

Kenzie planted her feet and stared directly into his eyes. "I'm going with you, and that's final. It's my life on the line, so I'm going."

"Well, it'll be my neck if anything happens to you."

She shrugged and looked as disinterested as she could.

Myles massaged the bridge of his nose and sighed loudly. "Listen, Kenzie, you can't go traipsing across the state with me, trying to figure out who wants you dead and why. To start with, they have to believe you're dead and that I'm out of the country, or they'll never relax enough to get caught."

She took a step toward him and was pleased with his slight recoil. "Myles, we're going to do this together or not at all."

"Not at all?" He grabbed his dark hair like he might rip it out by the roots. "You're insane! You don't get to make the decision on whether or not we—I mean, I—finish this assignment. I always complete my assignments. This won't be my first failure just because you want to be difficult."

"I'm not being difficult," she said, keeping her tone as soft and even as she could. Maybe she should have eased him into this discussion and to the understanding that she would be joining him. After all, she'd already made the decision. It was final.

Pacify him. His face is getting red, really red. Just pacify him.

"Maybe you're right. We should wait to make this decision until it has to be made. You're in no shape to be moved."

"Of course I'm right. Wait—but the decision has already been made. You're not coming with me. Period. End of conversation."

She smiled her sweetest smile. "Why don't you get some more sleep, and we'll talk when you get up."

He yawned loudly then furrowed his brow. "You're not coming. That's all there is to it. Nothing else to discuss."

"Get some rest and we'll talk," she said, smiling to herself.

Myles seemed unable to resist the sleep that once again claimed his body. He yawned again and mumbled something that she couldn't understand as his eyes closed and his head tilted back onto the small pillow.

His nap bought her a little bit of time, but she needed to think fast. When he awoke, she needed to be ready to present a fail-proof argument, something better than her own need to join him. Somehow, she was sure that her gut feeling would not be enough to persuade him. What could she possibly say that would convince him that she must go with him?

God, is this feeling from You? I know that I need to go with Myles, and I think You have something in store for us. Show me how I can convince him that this is Your plan to help me get safely home.

She sat quietly listening, waiting for peace, for something that assured her that she was following God's will.

When Myles finally woke hours later, Kenzie had her plan in place and the support from Lenora that she needed. While he had slept, Kenzie had explained as much as she could to the other woman.

"I knew he was up to something. But getting himself assigned to protect you from inside the prison? What a crazy scheme!"

she said as she unpacked the brown paper bag filled with groceries. "My grandson is either a very brave man or a fool."

Kenzie smiled. She definitely agreed he was one or the other. And if he didn't take her with him to investigate, he was definitely the latter. After laying out her reasons for needing to go with him, Kenzie asked Lenora, "So, you see why I have to go, right?"

"Of course I do. But I won't be able to convince him. You'll have to do that on your own."

"Oh, I will!" They remained silent for several moments before Kenzie could no longer contain the questions bombarding her mind. "How much did you know when Myles brought me to the cabin? Why didn't you try to help me? I thought you didn't care that I had been kidnapped. Why didn't you tell me that Myles is a special agent?"

Lenora smiled, patting Kenzie's shoulder affectionately. "Honey, I didn't know anything about your situation except that I trust my grandson. Myles is a good man, trustworthy and caring. I knew he intended you no harm, and I figured he'd tell you he works for the FBI when the time was right. Would you have been ready to hear it when you first arrived here?"

"Absolutely." Kenzie looked down at the thick socks on her feet. "Okay, maybe not right after we got here," she conceded.

Lenora nodded knowingly. "Myles is a lot like my Myles, my husband. He was a take-charge man, and I see him every time Myles gets that unwavering look in his eyes. I trust my grandson with my life, and I would trust him with yours, as well. When he's well enough to get out of that bed, he'll do what he's set out to do. He'll finish this assignment, and he'll keep you safe. After all, you already know he's willing to risk his life for you."

Kenzie swallowed thickly. She could barely manage to keep the burning at the back of her eyes from pouring tears down her cheeks. She wasn't sure when she had become such an emotional mess, but everything had happened so fast that she could barely keep her emotions in check.

Lenora's wrinkled hand squeezed hers. "You can trust him."

"Thank you."

Kenzie kept busy chatting with Lenora and helping her clean the little cabin as Myles napped into the evening. At almost ten o'clock, he groaned and turned to his left side, winced in his sleep, then rolled onto his back and groaned again. His eyes fluttered open then closed again.

While he was still half-asleep, Kenzie plopped down on the edge of the bed next to him and put her hands on his forearm.

"Myles," she whispered. He grunted, glaring at her through eyelids open just a slit. "Myles, I have to go with you."

"Nope. Don't even think about it. I'm taking you to the safe house outside of Portland so that everyone will think that you're dead, and I can go about figuring out who Whitestall was working for when he sent me after you."

She wanted to stamp her foot. He was far too alert for having just woken up. Her argument needed to be more persuasive than she'd thought. What to do? What to say?

He tried to tug his arm free from her grasp, but she clung to him. Somewhere deep in her heart she knew that having a physical connection with him would increase her chances of changing his mind. As an added bonus, she felt safer, more protected when she touched him.

"But won't you be recognized as an escaped prisoner?"

"I'll figure someth—" He stifled another yawn—and compelled to copy him, Kenzie yawned widely, too. "I'll figure it out."

"But wouldn't it be easier to have someone with you whose face isn't all over the news?"

His eyebrows furrowed for a moment and the left side of

his lips puckered. She was getting through to him. She just knew it. He was bound to understand her reasoning now. "Your face is probably in the news more than mine," he said. "Haven't you thought about how Mac will probably have your face plastered on every newscast, Internet site and milk carton across the country?"

Her jaw dropped. He was right. Why hadn't she considered that her family would be frantic with worry? Mac and Nana would be taking time from the campaign trail to hunt for her. They would make public pleas to her kidnapper for her safe return, completely unaware that no harm would come to her as long as she stayed with Myles. She had not even considered how this scenario would impact the people in her life.

She pictured Mac sitting at his enormous wooden desk at the capital building in Salem: He runs his large hand over his gray hair and studies the notes on a legal pad sitting before him. A knock on the door, and a young, naive clerk, face drawn tight, enters the office. The poor kid tells Mac that his only grandchild, the only child of his son who died more than twenty years before, Mac's own Kenzie, was kidnapped the previous night. Mac stands up so fast that his plush leather chair crashes to the floor, and he roars with anger. The poor clerk ducks his head and slips out the door.

Suddenly Kenzie let go of Myles's arm and covered her mouth with both hands. She didn't know whether to laugh or cry, and instead nearly choked on a hysterical sob. The entire crazy situation would make her lose her mind. She knew that look that she imagined on Mac's face. And she was certain that the image of that poor clerk was close to the reality.

Myles looked more than confused at the noise she'd released. He reached out a hand and rested it on her shoulder, but she turned from him.

"Are you okay?" he asked.

She couldn't respond through her emotional outburst.

"Kenzie. Talk to me. What's going on?" The mattress shifted as he wiggled to a sitting position.

When she could finally compose herself, she looked into his steady blue eyes and said, "Don't you understand how utterly crazy this entire situation is? My grandparents are probably frantic about my disappearance. I'm the only family they have left, and I've been kidnapped.

"I thought about leaving you—wounded—in the forest. But you saved my life, so I dragged you back to the cabin. Then you proceed to tell me that you're really an FBI agent. But even though you're a *good guy*—" she punctuated those two words with finger quotes in the air "—you're going to stash me away in a safe house and not let me contact my grandparents, who are likely going insane with worry."

He nodded stiffly.

"How am I supposed to react? It's all so crazy. I can't just sit back and do nothing while my family is worried to death about me. I have to do something to get us closer to the truth. Besides, you're trying to find someone who's after *me*. Wouldn't I be your best resource to find whoever has a grudge against me?"

Myles rubbed his hand over his face, his lips puckered and a look of disgust settled into his features. "We've been over this. I can't take you with me. It's not safe for you and it could hamper my investigation." He looked past her to Lenora, sitting in the rocking chair, knitting in front of the fire. "Grams, talk some sense into her. Please."

"I'm staying out of this, boy." She chuckled. "You two deserve each other."

"Could you do nothing while your only family worried about you?" Kenzie jumped in.

"Well, no. But this is different. It's my job to protect you."

Sending up one more quick prayer for just the right words to convince this stubborn man, Kenzie took a deep breath. "You said that we need to figure out who is spooking Larry, right? Well, I have an idea of where to start looking for answers."

"Where?"

"Not so fast. Promise me that I can go with you if you agree that it's a good idea."

"Fine!" Exasperation filled his voice.

A slow smile crept across her face. "Good. We start with Edna Whitestall."

"Edna Whitestall?" One eyebrow arched as he continued gazing steadily into her eyes.

"Edna Whitestall."

Kenzie hugged her arms tightly around her, slowly petting the soft cotton of her new shirt. While it was still technically a man's shirt, at least it was clean and new and didn't smell of mothballs. More importantly, it fit. In the it-still-made-her-look-like-a-man-but-that-was-the-idea sense of the word. She rubbed her nose into the navy blue collar and inhaled again.

She settled deeper into the front passenger seat of Lenora's white four-door sedan. Lenora had insisted they take it when they left the cabin. The police would be looking for Kenzie's car.

Kenzie was content for the moment in the parking lot of an Evergreen gas station. Except that Myles had been gone for more than four minutes. He'd promised to be back in five minutes, and she couldn't help the way her knee bounced incessantly. It seemed to know the importance of Myles's return.

A glance at her watch showed that he had exactly one minute left before she charged in after him.

Then a terrifying thought slammed into her mind. What if he left her? Or what if he had been caught?

All the money they had access to in the entire world was tucked into Myles's back pocket. Myles had laughed at her as she flipped through the worn Bible at the cabin. It held not only a treasure trove of wisdom and hope, but cash, too. When all the bills were counted, they had exactly four hundred and seventy dollars. It was enough for both of them to get by on, until they figured out who benefited from her demise.

But not if Myles did not return.

She peeked again at the tiny, independent store he had walked into four minutes and thirty-two seconds before. If he did not return, she needed a course of action.

But if he didn't return, would she ever be safe again? What if she was forced to spend her whole life looking over her shoulder? Never safe? Always on the run? No, that would be no way to live.

Just when she decided that she would see this ordeal through regardless of Myles's return, the driver-side door popped open and Myles folded his long legs under the steering wheel and started the engine in one smooth motion. Four minutes and fifty-two seconds. Right on time.

He quirked a smile at her and tossed her a plain, gray baseball cap, men's sunglasses and the daily newspaper.

"Well, let's see then," he rumbled.

"Oh!" She caught herself staring at his sleek T-shirt, also new, that hugged his chest and showed just enough of his sculpted bicep to tempt most women. It was a very good thing she was not most women.

Flipping her head forward, she tucked her hair beneath the cap then slid on the large sunglasses. "What do you think?"

He looked up from studying the single page in his hands and examined her carefully. "You look too...clean." He rubbed his chin with his thumb and forefinger. "You're missing a five o'clock shadow. Put some dirt on your face the next time we stop."

She crossed her arms in front of her chest. It was not her fault she couldn't grow a five o'clock shadow. Most women couldn't.

In this case she was very thankful to fall into the category of most women.

"Did you steal that page from the phone book in the gas station?"

He shrugged. "I borrowed it."

"Nice. Great example you're setting for the youth of America."

He snorted. "Youth of America, huh? And who exactly falls into the category? You?"

"Maybe not…but still! What happens when someone comes looking for the *W* page and it's gone? You're responsible for them not being able to find their friend."

"I'm also responsible for us finding Whitestall's mom."

"Oh." Not the world's best comeback, but it was good news. He'd done what he set out to do, and now they would be able to track down Edna Whitestall.

"Let's go meet Edna." He jammed the car into gear and floored it out of the parking lot and into traffic.

Myles drove like he did almost everything, with utmost confidence and coolness, and Kenzie found herself drawing from his assurance. As he weaved through traffic, she sat with her hands in her lap, not grasping the door handle as was her usual custom when driving with overly confident men.

In no time at all, they arrived on a street lined with identical houses in varying shades of natural brown, each lawn perfectly manicured and ready for guests', mailmen's or the homeowners association's inspection.

Kenzie looked down the street and her stomach sank.

"What's wrong?" Myles asked, distracted by the house numbers painted on the curb.

He must be a mind reader.

To him she said, "My condo is about four blocks that way." She pointed out her window. Home. It was so close. Her warm, comfortable bed. A phone from which she could call Mac and Nana.

"Well, put it out of your mind. That's the first place they'll look for us and the last place we need to be right now."

Myles pulled the car to the side of the street and parked between two other nondescript vehicles. In a flash, his arm slammed across her, and he clamped onto her tiny hand holding the handle to open her door.

"Wait. First we recon."

"Recon?"

"Reconnoiter. Survey. Explore. Scout. Investigate."

"I know what it means. But why are we recon-ing—reconnaissance-ing—reconnoitering? We need to get to Edna right away. She's got to help us figure out what's going on."

"First we make sure that we're not going to accidentally bump into Guard Whitestall. Then we see what data Ms. Whitestall wants to share with us."

"But won't she recognize—"

"Get down," Myles hissed, pushing her to the floorboard just in time to catch a glimpse of red and blue lights on top of a white sedan heading their way.

"What if they check the plates on Lenora's car? They'll know it's your grandma and they'll catch us!" If there was enough room between the seat and the dashboard, she would wring her hands.

Sitting as low as he could in the driver's seat, Myles said, "Don't worry. This car belongs to Lenora Borden, who is in no way related to the fictional Myles Parsons."

"Oh." Feeling like a squashed, rapidly blinking mushroom with back pain—do mushrooms have backs?—Kenzie elbowed her way out of the hiding place.

"Do you think the police officer recognized either of us?"

"No," he said. His eyes still panned the street. "You okay?"

"Sure. Why?"

He laughed. "You look like an old lady."

"I'm not old!"

"Sure. That's why you're rubbing your back. Because you're practically a kid."

"Practically," she mumbled. Searching for an excuse to ignore him, she snatched up the newspaper and immediately recognized the shot taking up half of the page above the fold.

Myles noticed it, too. "Nice picture. You look good."

Lord, please don't let her start crying. I can't handle that right now! I promised Grams that I would take care of her. That I wouldn't let her get hurt, physically or emotionally. I could really use a helping hand here. Please. Myles pleaded silently. Kenzie's eyes, stricken with something that looked like panic, never wavered from the page. His heart nosedived and he swallowed thickly, hating that she was hurting.

Please, oh, please let her keep that little crab shell she likes to put up. I know it's a facade, but I really need her to keep it together until we can get to a place where we can get some rest.

When silence had reigned almost longer than Myles could tolerate, he ventured to break into her thoughts. "What does it say?"

She blinked owl eyes at him, then looked back down at the newsprint. "They're pleading with you to return me, un-harmed. Th-they will give you anything you want. Mac is offering a hundred-thousand-dollar reward for my safe return."

"You know, for a hundred thousand dollars I could make a nice start in Mexico. You want to do it?"

Kenzie looked horrified. "Are you serious?"

"Why not? You'd be back with your family, and I'd have a hundred grand to spend on the Mexican beach, drinking little fruit smoothies out of coconuts with umbrellas in them."

"But…but…someone's trying to have me killed! And you just want to leave me? What about your job!"

He finally cracked a smile. "Oh, all right. I'll stay. For my job, of course."

"Jerk," she said almost under her breath, but the smile creeping onto her face tattled the truth.

"Yes. I probably am. So…is there anything about me in there?"

She flipped through several pages, her brow wrinkling. "Here's a little blurb about you on page five. How strange. They don't even have a picture of you in here. It just says that authorities believe that you may have already fled the country, and that Royal Canadian Mounties are on high alert and have promised to extradite you if you're discovered there."

"Not even a picture? I'm wounded!"

They shared a chuckle at his double meaning, and Myles was inordinately happy that she shared his humor, able to laugh in such a difficult circumstance.

Eventually, they settled into an amiable silence, Kenzie reading the newspaper, her knee bouncing up and down and Myles watching the house closely. It looked like every other house on the block: red-shingled roof, black mailbox with red flag, immaculate yard with a row of pristine flowers by the front door. Silver sedan in the driveway—some of the driveways sported SUVs, but all silver. Myles absently wondered if the homeowners association stipulated car color to keep the neighborhood uniform.

Just then a slight, frail-looking woman exited the front door of the house he watched so closely. Her grayish-white hair bounced and bobbed with her every step, and her flowery day dress billowed in the breeze as she shuffled around the side of the house.

She soon reappeared, dragging an enormous green garbage bin that looked like it might snap her tiny arm.

"Is that her?" he asked.

"Who?" Kenzie asked, still absorbed in her newspaper.

"Is that Edna Whitesall?"

Kenzie looked up quickly, gazing hard at the woman across the street. "I think so. I mean, I only met her once at the employee picnic. But it sure looks like her. And I think she might have been wearing the same dress."

"Good. Let's go have a chat."

"Wait! What if Larry comes back?" She put her hand gently on his forearm. A bolt of electricity passed through the simple touch, and he almost jumped out of the car. Did she feel that connection, too? She didn't remove her hand, but rather squeezed it tighter into his arm. Her lips pursed in a most becoming motion, and her eyes pleaded with him to be safe.

"He won't."

"But how do you know?"

"No woman that frail is going to take her own trash to the curb when her burly son is coming home that night. He's been gone long enough for her to know not to expect him home."

She looked uncertain, but finally let go of his arm. And he distinctly felt the loss of contact. "Okay, but we go together."

He nodded and they slipped from the car, making their way up the driveway, along the side of the silver sedan, coming into range of Edna Whitestall just as she reached for her front door.

"Mrs. Whitestall?" Myles called loud enough to catch her

attention. The old woman kept moving forward, oblivious to their presence or completely ignoring them. Her stuttered stride never faltering in her house shoes, she kept her head up and her gaze focused on the front door. Her slumped shoulders didn't twitch and she didn't make a sound.

"Mrs. Whitestall!" Kenzie tried. "Edna Whitestall! May we speak with you? Please!"

Still no response. She entered the house, closing the door behind her. Myles and Kenzie stopped on her front stoop and stared at each other. Kenzie looked as baffled as he felt. Finally he shrugged and pressed the doorbell button.

Several minutes passed with no response. But they wouldn't give up this easily. Myles pressed the pad of his index finger to the button, but stopped just shy of engaging the doorbell when the front door burst open.

There stood Edna, all wild, white hair and wind-blown cheeks. A black umbrella in her hands, resting against one shoulder, meant business. Myles took a sudden step back and reached back to push Kenzie behind him.

"Mrs. Whitestall?" When she gave no response, Myles plowed on. "I'm trying to find your son, Larry. Have you seen him lately?"

"I already told you lot! I have no comment!" Her voice sounded like a Doberman's bark coming from a Chihuahua.

"We're not from the press, ma'am," Kenzie offered from somewhere behind Myles's right shoulder. "We're just looking for Larry."

"Go away!" Edna howled, her eyes wild. Her knuckles white around the handle of her umbrella, she pulled it back and whacked Myles's shoulder. "I already told you, I'm not going to talk about it! But if you do see him, tell him that he needs to hurry home and clean out the garage."

Myles managed just an instant to survey the foyer of the

house. Pale oak floors. Antique mirror hanging above a small table, on which sat a canvas bag. Sticking out of the bag was some sort of bright red rubber. On the floor stood three stacks of newspapers, each a different height, in some kind of unusual sorting system. He expected to see a cat, as he could smell the litter box even from outside of the house. That explained why she had to take her trash out even without her son to help.

"Ye-yes, ma'am." He rubbed his shoulder and tried to hold back his laugh. This was some strange woman.

"Now, go away!" she yelled, slamming the door in their faces.

EIGHT

"I know that I should have taken her to the safe house, Nate. But she wouldn't go." Myles sighed heavily at the poor excuse he was giving his supervisor on the other end of the phone line. After relaying the entire story, from Whitestall coercing him to kill Kenzie to the mountain lion attack to their return to Evergreen, Myles was exhausted.

Special Agent in Charge Nate Andersen cleared his throat from his office in Portland. "There's nothing to be done about it now. You've put both of you in jeopardy, and you'll pay the consequences."

"Yes, sir."

"So what's your plan?"

"We didn't have any luck with Mrs. Whitestall today, but I know there's some information in that house about Whitestall. We'll try again tomorrow."

"All right. How are you doing for money?"

Myles almost laughed. Nate was barely a year older than Myles, but he still came across as a father figure most of the time. "Fine. I had almost five hundred stashed in the cabin, and we're doing okay on it. It should last at least a couple more days. Past that, I'll need you to wire us some money."

"Just let me know what you need. Take care of yourself

and stay in touch. Don't wait more than forty-eight hours to check in."

"Will do."

Myles hung up the phone and looked across the small hotel room where Kenzie sat with her back to him, her shoulders shaking slightly, but remaining silent. He ignored her for a moment, going back to the notes he'd written on the hand-size notepad emblazoned with the words *Evergreen Motel*, one of just a few motel choices in Evergreen. Despite Kenzie's looks of longing toward her condo, there was no way he would put her in serious danger just to return to a place that was comfortable. He would love to return to the cabin, but it was too far to drive back and forth. The information they needed to protect Kenzie and get his job done was in Evergreen. And all the information he had was scratched onto this little notepad.

His eyes roved over the notes.

Guard Whitestall. Whitestall's mom. Who else could be involved? Other guards? Superintendent Ryker? If so, how did they fit together? He drew circles around the names, drawing arrows among them, trying to make some kind of connection to the governor. How would hurting the governor help them? Did they really want to hurt the governor? Why else would they want to take Kenzie out of the picture? Was the intent to keep Governor Thorn from participating in the quickly approaching election?

None of it made much sense. There had to be an obvious connection. The problem was that it wasn't obvious to Myles.

He threw his pen onto the table next to his notepad and ran his fingers through his hair. He felt like growling. As the tension in his muscles built, he wanted to fight that mountain lion again. It would release some of the pressure building in him. But the painful twinge in his leg reminded him that he hadn't walked away from that battle unscathed. Even though he'd spent a day recovering in the cabin, the angry wound still seeped blood when he overexerted his leg. The pain was just another distraction from his main goal: protecting Kenzie. Another glance in her direction, and he could see from her posture that she was upset.

"Why don't you get some rest?" he asked her.

"Mmm-hmm."

"What?" he barked.

"Nothing," she choked, her voice breaking on a sob.

Great. Now he was taking his aggravation out on her. This was going to make their night better.

"Listen, I'm sorry. I'm not mad at you."

"Mmm." Then came the telltale sniffle.

No man knew what to do when confronted with a crying woman. Myles was certainly no exception to that rule. He put his chin on his chest and grumbled to himself. Why had he ever let her tag along? She should be at the safe house. Safe. And far away from him. Not getting under his skin when he least expected it.

She tried to muffle another sniff, and he knew that he could not ignore it forever. Squaring his shoulders, he walked around the beds until he stood in front of her.

Kenzie looked like a small child, wrapped in a too-large sweatshirt—a purchase from the secondhand clothing store— her red hair pulled back into a schoolgirl ponytail. Her shoulders slumped, and he could see light from the lamp reflected in the single tear making a silver track down her cheek, but she refused to take her eyes off of the patch of ugly brown carpet between her feet.

Myles sat down gently next to her, turning her body so he could look into her almost-closed eyes. They were stormy, like the ocean sky before a tempest.

"What's wrong?" His voice was almost a whisper, and he gently laid his hands on top of hers, which were folded in front of her.

She only shook her head in response, and still refused to meet his gaze.

"Let me help you fix it. Tell me what's wrong, and we'll figure out how to make it right."

"You'll laugh at me," she mumbled.

Why would he laugh at her? She was obviously upset.

"No, I won't."

She only nodded.

"Please, just tell me what's wrong. Is this about them? Do you miss your family? Is this about the article in the paper today?"

"It's so stupid." She hiccupped. "It's just…it's my birthday tomorrow. And I'm not going to be able to celebrate."

He couldn't help himself. Myles let out a loud snort. "Oh, sweetie!" He stood, and pulled her up, too. "Is that all?"

"I knew you'd think I was stupid!" Fire lit in her eyes, and she glared at him.

"I don't think you're stupid." He tried to smile without laughing, but her cute scowl brought a chortle from deep in his throat.

She shook her head and looked away, some of the fight leaving her stance. "Just leave me alone. Please."

Kenzie took a large step away from him. With his hands still firmly wrapped around hers, he gently tugged her back to a position standing before him. "I know I'm not your family, and I don't have any gifts for you, but I'll still celebrate with you."

"Really?" Her eyes opened wide. "What did you have in mind?"

He really had no idea, but he'd figure something out. And then the most absurd idea popped into his head. It was so ludicrous that he almost laughed out loud. But he couldn't stop himself.

"Well, there's something I could give you."

"I thought you didn't have any gifts."

Myles battled his conscience for a moment longer. She was in his care and protection, and he still had a job to do, a job that required him to keep a professional distance. If he followed his impulse, he would more than likely demolish any trust that she had in him.

She needs to be comforted.

But she needs to be able to trust me.

I'm sure she feels this electricity between us.

That doesn't give me any right to take advantage of her.

One look into the gray depths of her eyes, and he forgot any argument for not pulling her into a tight embrace. Before his common sense could object again, he hauled her into his arms. He saw her wild eyes and open mouth for just a moment before he closed his own eyes and pressed his lips to hers. She remained frozen for a moment, then yielded to his touch, wrapping her arms around his neck and resting her fingers in the shaggy hair at the nape of his neck.

His stomach nosedived, and he knew that his feelings for Kenzie Thorn had moved past fascination with her sweet-and-spicy personality. Could he really be falling for her?

Yes. And if he wasn't careful he would fall hard.

Oh, he was still more than content with bachelorhood, its freedom and independence. After all, married agents were usually stuck with desk jobs. They rarely asked for field assignments, and they missed out on the adrenaline of living in the moment, the best part of the job.

For the briefest moment, the idea of a life with a woman flickered across his imagination. It wasn't as though he'd never thought of what it would be like to settle down, to get married. But his previous daydreams were always with a faceless woman. Suddenly she had a face. Relaxing Saturday mornings, lounging around their Portland house. Random emotional outbursts. Cooking dinner together, then eating across the table, sharing the simple joys of the day. Wild fits of laughter. Racing through forests. Saving her from wild animals. Sweet, red-haired babies. Desk job or not, life with sweet-and-spicy Kenzie would never be boring.

After a few moments, she pulled away and looked at him with slightly hooded eyes. He smiled at her, cupping her cheek with his hand. A single teardrop still slid down her cheek, and he swiped at it with his thumb.

"Happy birthday." Her smile wavered tremulously. "Crawl into bed and get some sleep. I'll be back in the morning."

"Where are you going?" she mumbled.

"Don't worry. I'll be back in the morning."

She did as she was told, sliding into the bed. Within moments her breathing evened to a steady rhythm, and then he slipped out the hotel room door. He had to close the door to the room and to the crazy thoughts Kenzie brought him.

Kenzie woke with a start. What a wonderful dream she had just had. Myles held her to his chest and kissed her full on the mouth. Her lips tingled slightly now, and she pressed the tip of her middle finger to her lower lip. In her dream she'd never felt so protected, so secure.

"You awake?"

Myles's voice made her jump, and she sat straight up in bed, hands immediately going to her hair to try to resume some order there.

"Happy birthday." He stood beside her bed, holding out a small donut with a single pink candle in it. "I know it's probably not like your grandma's birthday cake or anything, but it's the best I could do."

"Thank you." She reached out to take the little paper plate

from him, her gaze only able to zero in on his lips. In real life, did he kiss like he did in the dream? One could only hope.

"My pleasure."

And suddenly those perfect lips moved forward and landed on hers. There was no warning, no preparation, just that sensational feeling of electricity passing between them. "One more for your special day," he whispered.

One more? So it wasn't a dream!

Still lost in her brief joy, Kenzie almost missed the solemn expression that rolled across his face, replacing his smile. He shrugged once, shook his head and said, "Come on. We've got to go see what's going on with Edna."

Tingling from head to toe, she jumped up and followed him, still holding her birthday donut close to her heart.

How could she possibly have thought that the kiss the night before was a dream? Now that she was wide-awake, she wanted to recall every detail, every moment of being in his arms. The way his dark hair fell across his forehead. The way the soft tendrils of his hair felt like silk to her fingertips. The way he smelled like a man, freshly showered, redolent of soap and shampoo. The way he hadn't demanded or pushed her for more than she was willing to give. Heaven on earth.

Caught up in her own world of memories, she lagged behind, staring blindly up at the puffy white clouds floating lazily through the sky.

"Thorn! Let's go!" Myles's voice was both quiet and firm.

Myles stood with one leg in the car, resting his arm on the car door. He looked less than pleased with the delay.

"Sorry," she said as she slipped into the passenger seat. How could he ruin such a pleasant memory for her with his impatience today? It would serve him right if he never got to kiss her again. "And since when did you start calling me Thorn?"

"Since today."

"Are you mad at me?" she said.

"No. Just focused on the mission."

"You sure didn't feel that way ten minutes ago with your repeat of last night."

"It was just to cheer you up for your birthday. It won't—can't—happen again. We can't get distracted today." The muscles in his jaw jumped. The vein at the base of his throat pulsed wildly.

His sudden intensity seemed out of the character that she knew, and impulsively she wanted to get back at him. "Well, that's all well and good, but you've just guaranteed yourself to never have a revisit of that kiss!" And then it was hanging out there. *Kiss.* It was just an ordinary word, not dirty or terrible.

But that one word hung between them for an eternity, like a never-ending verbal reminder of the intimate moment they shared.

Kenzie could feel the heat rising up her neck, and she suddenly clamped her hands on her cheeks, as if to stop the movement of the rogue blush.

Myles ducked his head and broke their eye contact. "I'm sorry, Kenzie. I just get a little wound up before an assignment. I shouldn't take it out on you."

She nodded and finally became fully aware of the uncomfortable lump pushing into her back. With a little tug, a pillow in a white case popped out from behind her, and she almost screamed as she flung it away from her.

"Why do you have a pillow in the car?"

Nonchalantly, he pulled the car out of its parking spot and pulled into moving traffic. "I brought the pillow from the cabin."

"But why?"

"Because I like to sleep with a pillow."

She cocked her head and stared at him. "You slept in the car?"

He did not respond immediately; instead, he seemed intently focused on the red light directly ahead of him while chewing his lower lip. Kenzie wondered why she'd never noticed that trait before. It couldn't be nerves that were keeping him from speaking.

The silence answered her question, so she asked another. "Why did you sleep in the car? You need to be able to stretch your leg out. It'll never heal if you keep using it and don't let it rest."

"My leg is fine."

"But why?"

He opened his mouth wide, then snapped it shut. After a long silence, he spoke very softly. "I just don't think it's a good idea for a man and a woman to share a room—motel or other—if they're not married." She wholeheartedly agreed, and had been pleased she hadn't had to ask him to leave the room the night before. "I needed to make sure you were safe, and I couldn't watch the room from another room. It was easy enough to keep tabs on you from the car."

And just like that Myles earned himself a repeat of that kiss they'd shared the night before. Oh, she'd wait to give it to him, but it would definitely happen. Now that he'd shown that he cared enough not just to protect her life, but her reputation, as well, he'd earned a repeat.

Just now she refrained from throwing herself at him and put one of her hands over his instead, all of his earlier comments forgiven. "Thank you, Myles. I think that may be the most thoughtful birthday present I've ever received."

Myles squeezed her hand gently and shot her a quick smile, as he pulled onto a small side street that Kenzie immediately recognized.

"So, are you going to eat that donut?"

Kenzie realized that she hadn't touched her chocolate-frosted donut with pink and blue sprinkles. It sat idly on her leg, looking like some crazy adornment on her new jeans.

New jeans and a donut. New clothes—well, new to her—all around, *and* a donut. Life was good.

Really good.

"You should put your hat and sunglasses on. I have a feeling this neighborhood gets patrolled quite a bit. That cop we saw yesterday will likely be back."

She mumbled incoherently, chewing a large bite of donut. She swallowed noisily, then tried again. "I will. Just a minute."

Licking her fingers and delighting in every savory taste, she sighed loudly, suddenly regretting the urgency with which she ate the donut. The only donut.

"Hat."

She reached behind her and scraped her hand on the underside of the seat and finally made the hat and sunglasses appear. Pressing them into place, she noticed how intently Myles studied the house across the street.

"What are you thinking?"

"I'm not sure," he mumbled.

"Well, that's reass—"

He held up his hand for silence, and she obliged. "I think that the answers to most of our questions about Whitestall are probably on the other side of that door."

"So?"

"So we need to get in there."

"But what about Edna Whitestall? I don't think she's going to suddenly decide to help us after she beat you up with her umbrella yesterday."

"First, she did not beat me up." His eyes blazed with something less than anger and more like humor. "Second, she's not home."

"How do you know?"

"Her car is gone, and so is almost everyone else's on the block."

Something niggled at the back of Kenzie's brain. She'd seen something the day before, pertinent information. But what was it? "I saw something…yesterday. Umm…I just can't remember."

"What are you talking about?" His eyes sweeping back and forth up the street.

She gritted her teeth and tried to concentrate. "The newspaper!"

Plunging an arm into the backseat, she groped for the folded-up paper on the floor behind the driver's seat. She spun forward, newspaper in hand, scanning the pages as quickly as she could.

"'Rash of robberies.' 'Governor's race closer than expected,'" she mumbled the headlines as she flipped the pages. "There!" Kenzie pointed at a spot on the events page. Myles had stopped watching the road and was looking at her with both wonder and concern. He finally dipped his head to read the three-line activity announcement.

"YMCA seniors swimming! Of course! I saw a bag in her house yesterday that must be her swim bag. It had a red swim cap sticking out of it."

"Swim cap? Sounds fashionable."

He chuckled. "Grams used to wear one every time she took us swimming when I was kid."

"Ri-ight."

He only smiled and looked again at the listing. "Well, it looks like the whole neighborhood is at the YMCA community center for swimming and water aerobics for another forty-five minutes. I guess we'd better get going."

"Where are we going?"

"I've got an idea, but we need to get some necessary items to get inside when Edna gets back."

"What do we need?"

Myles pulled back onto the major street and headed back toward the secondhand store they'd visited before. "If Edna's going to let me into her house, then I have to look the part."

NINE

An hour later, Myles watched Kenzie disappear around the corner of the house and then waited several seconds. Then he knocked loudly on Ms. Edna's screen door, rattling the entire frame. Adjusting his recently purchased, secondhand electrician's shirt, he straightened his shoulders.

This entire idea was doomed to fail, but they had to try. It was the only idea they had to get inside Edna's house and figure out what her son knew.

For a moment he closed his eyes and prayed fervently for favor. *God, please keep Kenzie and me safe. Show us where we need to go to find whatever information Whitestall might know. Father, you know my desire is to serve You and protect Kenzie. Please give me the wisdom to do both.*

After what seemed like an eternity, shuffling steps sounded from the opposite side of the door, and Edna's white hair and wrinkled face appeared on the other side of the screen. She squinted at him, and he tugged on the bill of his baseball cap, praying she wouldn't recognize him from the day before.

"What do you want?" Her voice was like gravel and her eyes like flint.

Myles closed his eyes and sent up one more quick prayer for favor in finding what they needed inside Edna's house.

"Hello, ma'am. We've heard about some possible gas leaks in the area. Would you mind if I checked your furnace line to make sure there isn't a problem?"

Edna glared at him so long that he was sure she would refuse. Then she finally reached out and unlocked the screen door. Not bothering to open it for him, she nodded her head down the short hallway, making her way toward the back of the house. Myles jumped into action, following closely behind her and silently thanking God for her acquiescence.

"Make it fast," she said, at the top of a short flight of stairs. "I was just heading out the door." Her eyes were stern, and he had the distinct impression that she had nowhere pressing to be. She just didn't want him in her house any longer than absolutely necessary.

Myles took a quick glance around the kitchen and into the disaster that could only be Larry's room just off the kitchen. Then he nodded and hurried down the steps, thankful that she didn't follow behind him. Hurrying to one of the high basement windows, he quickly unlocked it and pushed it open. Immediately Kenzie's feet popped through the opening. He grabbed her waist as she slid through and landed easily on the floor.

He quickly jiggled the gas line attached to the furnace, twisting the line slightly.

"What are you doing?" Kenzie asked, her face a mask of bewilderment.

"Making sure she really doesn't have a gas leak." Shooting a smile at Kenzie, he hurried back to the stairs. His feet landed silently on each step as he crept toward the door to the rest of the house. Suddenly Edna appeared on the landing, her hands firmly planted on her hips.

"How much longer?"

"It's going to be a little while. I was just coming to let you know. Your line was a little loose, and I want to make sure it's secure. Would you like me to light your pilot while I'm here?" Myles silently shot a prayer toward the ceiling that Kenzie had ducked out of view and was invisible to Edna's prying eyes.

"Make it fast!" she snapped, turning on her heel.

Myles turned back to Kenzie as she slipped from around the concrete corner of the wall. He put his finger to his lips and listened to Edna's footsteps moving toward the far corner of the house.

Finally he whispered, "Stay behind me until we hit the landing. Then get into Larry's room as fast as you can. Dig around in there until I come get you. If you hear Edna, hide."

Kenzie looked doubtful, but finally nodded her acquiescence, her eyes huge in the dim light. He felt only a twinge of guilt over sending her into the untidy room, but he doubted that anyone would be able to find anything in the pig sty. Plus, she could be as careless as she liked, and no one would ever be able to tell anyone had been snooping in that room. He needed to look carefully at the rest of the house, unhindered by a walking shadow.

He turned and hurried toward the kitchen landing, his eyes peering into every corner, trying to get the lay of the land. Immediately pushing Kenzie into the pig sty, he hurried silently around the kitchen.

He turned to look for the trash can, tripping over a four-legged fur ball. His heart jumped to his throat in surprise. "Great, I'm scared of fluffy white cats," he grumbled silently as he pushed the cat away with his leg and moved to the trash can. Empty, the bag just replaced. No scraps of paper or notepads lying around. Everything in its proper place. The kitchen would be little help. Keeping an ear open, he crept down the short hallway toward the front door. He passed another hallway, leading toward two more doors, one closed, the other ajar. He figured that was Edna's bedroom, and probably where she was at that moment.

In the foyer he spotted what he'd been looking for. Just where he had seen them the day before sat the three stacks of newspapers. They tugged at his imagination, conjuring images of all kinds of crazy reasons for a woman to keep such a collection of newspapers. He doubted they had anything to do with Kenzie's kidnapping—there were too many to have accumulated in the few short days since his prison escape—but maybe they could clue him into something about the missing prison guard.

He knelt on the floor next to the largest stack and quickly scanned the first page. A headline about halfway down the page announced that the governor's race was closer than anyone expected. Another article condemned the gubernatorial candidates, including Judge Claudia Suarez for running accusatory and unfounded advertising campaigns.

Rifling through the stacks, he found only newspapers from Mondays, and they went back more than a year.

What could possibly be so special about Mondays? Will she take tomorrow's paper and add it to her stacks? He mentally talked himself through the piles of papers.

Deep in thought, he almost missed the tiny creak of the floorboards.

Movement down the hallway!

Oh-crud-oh-crud-oh-crud-oh-crud! Shoving the stacks of papers back into formation and racing down the hallway, he slid past Edna as she backed out of her bedroom, closing the door behind her. *Thank You, God, for that little favor.*

Keeping his footfalls silent, he raced into the bedroom where Kenzie hid. Just as he slid past the door and closed it most of the way, his mountain lion wound screamed in pain. Looking down, he noticed the metal bed frame that had connected with his injury. He chomped on his lower lip to keep from hollering with the agony.

His eyes sought out Kenzie's across the room. She poked her questioning eyes above the unmade bed. He just shook his head and again pressed his forefinger to his lips. Kenzie nodded as Edna puttered into the kitchen.

Footsteps approached the door, and a hand clamped onto his forearm. Myles looked into Kenzie's anxious gray eyes. Her clean, fresh scent surrounded him. Kenzie's little hand let go, then immediately reconnected with his forearm as she clung to him. Silence hung in the air, but she spoke through little squeezes of her fingers. As slow footsteps moved closer to the cracked door, she squeezed tighter. If he could see her knuckles, he was sure that they would be white. A shadow blocked the light coming from the kitchen, and he was certain they were doomed. But her grip relaxed as the footfalls moved farther into the kitchen.

And then the worst possible thing happened. Ms. Edna picked up the telephone. One beep, as she punched in the first number. Two. Three. Four, five, and six. Please, just one more. Beeps seven and eight. Nine and ten. A long distance call.

Myles groaned inwardly and clutched the knee of his suddenly shaking leg with the hand that wasn't occupied as Kenzie's squeeze toy. He clamped his hand over his thigh and felt the sticky ooze through his pant leg. Suddenly his head began spinning, and he had to lean his chin on his chest and close his eyes.

He could hear Edna talking on the phone, but could make out nothing she said over the rushing in his ears. Her footsteps worked their way from one wall to another in the kitchen, and in his mind's eye he could see her pacing to the end of the curly phone cord and then stretching it in the other direction. With her right on the other side of the door, they were trapped.

And who knew for how long?

After several minutes of silence, Kenzie leaned in until her lips brushed his ear. "Are you okay?" He nodded in response but could not summon the strength to speak at the moment. Clammy with sweat, he leaned into her shoulder. Then her arm slipped around his shoulder, and she rested one cool hand on his forehead.

"Are you sure you're okay?" her voice almost inaudible but strong.

"Yes."

"You're weak. What's wrong?"

How on earth could she know that something was wrong? There was no way she could see his leg in the darkness, though the reopened wound on his right leg howled in pain at just the thought of it. "I'm bleeding again."

TEN

Kenzie's hand brushed the sticky mess on Myles's thigh and she instinctively pulled back, biting her tongue to keep from crying out at the amount of blood she felt there. No wonder he was leaning so heavily against her shoulder. She had to stop the blood before he left a mess for Edna Whitestall to find later. More importantly, she had to stop the blood before Myles was too far gone to be any help.

And she needed help right now.

Reaching around her on the pile of dirty clothes on the floor, she hunted for something to tie around the leg to stop the blood flow. Nothing. She could tear her shirt sleeves, but that would cause too much noise. Even now Edna marched just on the other side of the door, making a ruckus in the kitchen.

Her hand landed on her waist, and therein lay the help she needed. Unbuckling her belt as fast as she could with one hand, she pulled it free from the belt loops and nudged Myles awake.

"I need you to help me."

He grunted softly. "What?"

"Help me tie this around your leg so you don't lose any more blood."

With fumbling fingers he held on to one end of the belt as Kenzie tugged the other end under his leg and wrapped it around. They managed to get it tight enough that he grunted again, this time in pain.

Myles's breathing eased slightly, and she took several moments to rescan the room. Immediately, her eyes landed on the prison guard uniform crumpled almost underneath the bed, that she'd missed during her first look around the room. Clearly, it had been waiting to be laundered for quite some time. Could it contain some bit of information that she had not found in the rest of the room? Obviously unsavory things were happening at the prison, if that's where Larry had conscripted Myles. Maybe the others behind this plot were at the prison, as well.

Leaning Myles against the wall behind them, she peeked out the door and slipped across the floor to rifle through the pile of clothes. Tucking her fingers into every pocket, she found thirty-four cents, a paper clip, some lint and a little sticky note. Squinting at the block print on the paper, she made out the words, *"Call when the job is done,"* followed by a phone number, and signed *"Joe."*

Suddenly Myles groaned, and she looked up just in time to see his eyes droop closed again. Hopping back to his side, she said, "Wake up, Myles. Talk to me."

"About what?" he whispered.

She wasn't sure. How much noise could they make? Edna was just on the other side of the door, and if they weren't careful they'd give themselves away. And then—as if in response to Kenzie's unprayed prayer—Edna's words clearly rang through the door.

"My hearing aid is bothering me again. I'm going to take it out, so you just speak up really clear now… What? Speak up!"

Kenzie smiled and silently thanked God for knowing exactly what they needed. Then she whispered to Myles, "Anything. Tell me where you went to school."

"School?· I went to Kofa High. I played on the football team. We weren't great, but we won city my senior year."

The smile in his soft voice filled the small room. "Go on. What about college?" Silence reigned for several moments until she thought he hadn't heard her. "College?" she prompted.

"I…I wanted to be a navy SEAL. Always. I just wanted to be part of that elite team, to belong to something bigger than myself. I spent my entire time in high school just preparing to join the navy. I never worried about college. I was going to be a SEAL.

"And then, during the city championship game my senior year, I got tackled, and my ACL was shredded. A couple of surgeries and I was supposed to be good as new, so they let me join the navy. I made it through boot camp and then registered for SEAL training as soon as I could. I was in the best shape of my life and passed all of the exams with flying colors, but then I had a physical just before BUDs—"

"Buds? What's that?"

Myles rubbed his left knee absently in a gentle rotating motion. "Basic Underwater Demolition—the training program for SEALs. Its core is an eight-week intensive conditioning program that culminates in the worst week on the planet. Sleep-deprived, hungry, every muscle aching, pushing yourself past every limit you thought you had. Man, it would have been great!"

"Sounds like a blast."

"Yeah, well, it's all I ever wanted. But the doctor didn't pass me. He wouldn't let me even attempt BUDs. Said it would be too hard on my knee. Said I'd never walk again if I reinjured it, and there was a strong likelihood of that during training.

"So I finished out my four-year enlistment. Sadly, I was less than a model seaman." She willed him to open up more, to share the details. She wanted to see his heart, to know what his life before this moment was really like.

"I barely managed to keep my name off a list of men court martialed for conduct unbecoming a member of the U.S. Navy. I was angry and still just looking to belong to something bigger than myself. I needed a new goal, a new purpose, and until I found it, I was only about having a good time.

"My uncle used to be in the secret service, so I thought about that, but it didn't seem a good fit for me. I wanted more than just standing on the sidelines of history."

While he swallowed, Kenzie heard Edna talking loudly, still in the kitchen. Her words jumbled together, but there was a definite cadence to the way Edna spoke. A chair scraped along the linoleum and a loud sigh echoed into the adjoining room.

"It was my mom who suggested the FBI. She said she'd been praying for me and that she was sure I was supposed to be a special agent. I laughed at her at first. I really hadn't had anything to do with God since I was forced to go to youth group in high school. But that seed was planted, and when I started college at the University of Arizona, courtesy of the G.I. Bill, I was already seriously thinking about law enforcement. Three of the five courses I took my first semester were political science and criminal justice classes. After that, I was hooked.

"It took me three years to get my bachelor's, working straight through, another two years for law school at Arizona State, and by then I was sure that the FBI was the right place for me. I'd cleaned up my act and stayed on the right side of the law, and I thought that joining the bureau would give me the sense of belonging that I'd always wanted."

"And it didn't?"

Sighing even more heavily into Kenzie's shoulder, he shook his head. She felt the brush of his soft hair against her cheek. "No. It didn't. I loved the bureau right away, but I was still lost. I didn't fit in. I was missing something. I knew it, and I was beginning to realize that I wasn't going to find it in the SEALs or the bureau or school or anywhere else.

"When I was stationed in the Portland field office, I met this woman, Heather. She invited me to her church. I must have turned her down at least a dozen times. But she had this beautiful blond hair, and I had this idea that if I just went to church with her, maybe she'd go on a date with me."

Kenzie saw green for a moment, instantly despising Heather and her gorgeous hair. Her shoulders twitched and her hands fisted into Myles's shirt. He winced, and she realized she had grabbed more than just his shirt. Trying to tamp down her wayward emotions, she focused on Myles's whispers.

"Anyway, things with Heather never went anywhere—"

Kenzie let out the breath she didn't even realize she had been holding in.

"—but I got hooked on the church. The people there just seemed to really care about me and each other. This older couple, the Stirlings, invited me to their house for lunch after church on my second Sunday there. They became like another set of grandparents to me, and Roger helped me through the death of my grandparents—my mom's parents—a couple years ago. I wanted to be just like him.

"Don't get me wrong, my parents are great, and my grandparents were wonderful. But there was something so incredibly contagious about Roger. It was the way he greeted everyone like he'd known them for a lifetime. The way he listened when I talked, even about the most mundane things. The way he still held his wife's hand after forty-five years of marriage. I wanted what he had."

Even the forty-five years of marriage? A scene of Myles's eighty-year-old hand covered in age spots and little tufts of white hair, holding her equally wrinkled hand, flashed before her eyes.

"I guess I'd always known that I couldn't—wouldn't—have any of that unless I really decided what I was going to do with God. So, when my grandparents passed away so close together, I took it as a reminder that none of us are guaranteed one more day on this earth. I found that God had been waiting for me, so close, right there all the time, waiting for me to turn to Him."

Kenzie blinked at the wetness in her eyes, fighting the urge to wipe them. She cleared her throat as softly as she could, not sure what to say.

And suddenly she didn't have to respond to what Myles had said.

"Did you hear that?" she whispered.

He nodded. A door had definitely opened. Edna must have left the kitchen while Kenzie was consumed with Myles's story.

"I'm going to go check it out." She leaned him back against the cool wall, then hopped up and hurried to the crack in the door. Silence. She held her breath, waiting for something, anything. She reached behind her and pulled Myles to his feet, letting him rest on her shoulders.

Then a toilet flushed.

Doing her best impression of Myles, she cleared her throat and said, "All set, ma'am. No leaks. You should be good to go for the winter. Have a good day."

Ignoring the heaviness of the dead weight around her shoulders, Kenzie raced for the nearest exit, the back door. Hobbling around the side of the house, they burst into the open side yard.

At the curb she looked left. Clear. Looked right.

Police car.

A white car with red and blue lights pulled to a stop in front of them!

Myles took a twisted step from the soft, lush grass to the firm cement of the sidewalk. His leg howled, and black spots obstructed his vision. Blinking rapidly, he clung to the slim shoulders under his left arm.

When his vision finally cleared, he began to sigh—but stopped in an almost hiccup.

The police car rolled toward them, silent but deadly. If they were captured, he could do nothing to protect Kenzie, to save her from whoever had risked everything to take her out of the picture. And he'd fail his assignment, too, which of course was the real issue. Right?

Kenzie's right arm squeezed at his middle, and he chanced a look down at his left leg. A dark red stain marred his new jeans, and he realized that he would have to do some fancy talking to get them out of this.

Claiming an attack of some sort would only spur the police officer to greater interest. An emergency too severe would mean too many questions. He had to offer just the right excuse for why two men—after all, this officer should see Kenzie as a man—ran from a backyard, one with blood coming from his leg and the other holding his friend up.

A chance glance at the soft facial lines and smooth jaw of the woman next to him and he knew the jig was up. No way would any man with a pulse mistake Kenzie for anything other than what she truly was.

The police car pulled up to the curb directly in front of them, and the passenger-side window rolled down with a slight hissing noise.

"Afternoon, gentlemen." The police officer was young, with classic but forgettable features, his hair slicked back with more oil than his sedan probably used in a month.

Myles opened his mouth, but was immediately cut short.

"Afternoon, officer." The voice that came from Kenzie's lips was rough and slightly hoarse, and Myles almost didn't recognize who had interrupted him.

The officer rested on his steering wheel with one arm and leaned so far toward them that his face nearly eclipsed the passenger door. "What seems to be the trouble here?"

"Oh, my stupid cousin stabbed himself in the leg with Aunt Edna's gardening shears." She nudged Myles in the rib. "We was working on cleaning out her garage. Ever since Larry took off, she hasn't had much help around the house."

The officer looked down. "I was really sorry to hear that Larry took off. We sure like Ms. Edna. Any word where he might have gone or why?"

Kenzie shook hear head vigorously. "Nope. Just got sick of the place, I guess." Myles cringed. He had a good idea why Whitestall had taken off. Their one and only phone call was the likely culprit. The guard had been wondering the same thing as Myles—what reason would the man behind the plot to kill Kenzie have for keeping his pawn alive? No reason to keep him around—and a lot of good ones to get rid of him, too. Whoever this mastermind was, he hadn't immediately revealed himself. He was smarter than a lot of criminals, and he wouldn't leave loose ends. The guard was a loose end. He knew too much.

Myles was sure Whitestall had run out of sheer self-preservation.

"Do you want me to call for an ambulance?"

"Naw." Kenzie hiked up her pants and jabbed Myles in the ribs again. He'd never been so thankful to be poked. She was in character and completely in control of this situation. He'd seen her spitting mad and cool and collected since the kidnapping, but he hadn't seen her *this* in control since she taught a room full of convicted felons. "It was just a scratch. We used the first-aid kit in Aunt Edna's bathroom and tied a belt around his leg. I'm just going to take him back to the hotel and let him sleep for a while."

"All right. Well, drive safe."

The officer pulled his car from the curb and drove slowly down the street.

Kenzie waited several seconds, then dragged Myles across the road and shoved him into the backseat of her car. He bumped his head on the car frame and fell like a rag doll onto the upholstery. He pulled his knees to his chest as quickly as he could, to avoid losing a foot in the slamming door.

She yanked open the front door and huffed into the driver's seat. "Keys." It was a demand.

He dug in his jeans pocket and handed them to her. He couldn't help the smile that tugged at the corner of his lips.

Ah, the return of Spicy Kenzie.

She missed the ignition hole with the key and shoved at it again. It banged into place and she revved the engine before practically squealing the tires.

"Nice work there with the cop." He tried to fill the silence, to help her calm down.

Her reflection glared at him through the rearview mirror. "No thanks to you!" she spat.

"You were amazing! Where did you come up with that story?"

"Quit trying to make nice! You—you—you got yourself reinjured and left me to fend for the both of us. And you made me lie! I hate lying! How dare you!"

The adrenaline from the run-in with the cop was likely taking over her emotions, causing her to lash out at him. Kenzie yanked the wheel to the right, then the left, swerving in and out of the busy lanes of traffic.

Myles swallowed the lump in his throat and blinked at unexpected wetness in his eyes. The pain vanished, and he could only focus on the enormous, stormy-gray eyes that reflected back to him in the rearview mirror. And then he noticed the liquid pooling at the inside corners of her eyes.

"Kenz, pull over."

Her nostrils flared, and her left eye squinted, as it was apt to do when she was this upset.

"Kenzie. Pull over. We can't afford to be in an accident and have another meeting with a cop."

She glared at him again, but pulled into the parking lot of a grocery store and turned the car off.

Fighting through the pain, Myles worked to free himself from the backseat. He wiggled left, bringing searing pain, wiggled right—slightly less pain.

Finally, he stood outside Kenzie's door and tugged it open. He ignored his spinning head. Pulling her to her feet, he blocked her against the car and cupped her face with his palms. Her eyes darted around the parking lot, looking at anything but him.

"Kenzie," he whispered softly. "I'm going to do my best to protect you. I'm not leaving you anytime soon."

"But you were—you were so heavy and…and you are still bleeding."

"Forget about the leg. I'm fine. A little weak. In need of a new Band-Aid, maybe. But I'm fine."

She still refused to look into his face, even as he brushed a tear from her cheek. "I was—I was afraid that I'd lose you. That we'd be caught. That that cop would see right through me and that crazy story. I was so afraid—"

Myles could not make out the rest of the words that she mumbled, as she flung her arms around his waist and tucked her face into his neck. He simply rubbed his hands in small circles over her shoulder blades and whispered nonsense into her hair.

When she finally pulled back and met his gaze, she smiled tremulously. "I'm sorry I just broke down on you." She tapped the damp spot on his shirt and made a funny face.

"It's okay. I'm sorry I took you into that house." He glared at his shoes. "I guess it was a waste of time. I thought for sure there would be some useful information in there."

And maybe if I'd spent less time on dead-end stacks of newspapers, we'd have found it.

"Well, it wasn't a complete waste of time."

"I know. Now we know a slightly crazy woman lives there."

A crazy woman who puts newspapers out like a red herring, just waiting for Special Agent Borden to fall for it.

Kenzie dug into the front pocket of her jeans and held out her hand. A small scrap of yellow paper sat in her palm. "We know Joe, and we know a phone number."

ELEVEN

Kenzie pulled her car into the parking lot of a small motel on the corner of Main and Jewel Drive. "The Jewel" claimed vacancies at only $29.99 per night.

"What are you doing?" Myles mumbled from the backseat.

Glancing at his still form filling the entire backseat, Kenzie parked the car and opened her door. "I'm going to get you a room. You need to get some rest so you can stop bleeding." She flashed him a smile. "I'm sick of you getting blood all over Lenora's car. So just sit still for a second. I'll be back."

She hurried toward the front office. Her face and arms flushed with the heat of the late summer day. Yanking open the glass door, she walked into a wall of humidity. Her hope for a short reprieve denied, Kenzie sucked in a shallow breath and hunched her shoulders, creating room between her skin and the lightweight cotton of her shirt.

A man with a brown mustache and no other hair on his head sat on the opposite side of a plastic partition that ran the length of the counter. Circular dirt smudges covered the tan countertop, and Kenzie resisted the urge to lean on it.

"Help you?" the ogre on the other side of the counter grunted. He stood, showing off his wide girth. His white T-shirt sported yellow stains around his neck and under his arms, and he sucked at his front tooth, the sound grating for even well-rested nonfugitives. Bloodshot eyes roamed from her knees to the secondhand baseball cap.

Kenzie's muscles tensed and she physically restrained herself from shuddering. "Sure. I need a room for me and a friend."

"Just the one night?"

"For now."

"You know we rent for shorter periods than the night." He glanced pointedly from Kenzie to her car.

She couldn't contain a full-body shudder this time. Nostrils flaring, she reached into her pocket and produced two twenty-dollar bills. "Just one full night for now."

The man shrugged and handed her a key and her change through the opening in the partition. "Number three. Around the corner. Third door."

Kenzie nodded and backed away from the man, too disgusted to turn her back on him. When she reached the door, she almost sprinted to the car, then slammed the door shut. Every motion jerky and rushed, she pulled the car around to the side of the single-story building.

Myles somehow seemed to know her discomfort, so he made the transition from the car to the motel room using as little assistance as he could. His feet shuffled along the sidewalk until she fumbled with the key in the door of room three.

When the door flew open, they stumbled inside and Myles flung himself on the only bed in the room. He rolled over onto his back, sighed loudly and instantly began snoring.

Kenzie smiled to herself as she closed the crusty curtains, attempting to block some of the glaring sunlight, and fiddled with the air conditioner. Unlike every other hotel room she had ever stayed in, the air conditioner was not turned on full-blast. All of the markings on the unit had long since been rubbed away, so she twisted the knobs until it gave a tremble and then hissed out lukewarm air.

The room was small with one double bed. A round table with a single chair sat in the far corner, and the strong smell of stale smoke permeated every corner. A tiny television that looked older than Kenzie sat on what looked like a TV tray in the corner adjacent to the table and chair.

"Well, maybe we'll be able to watch some news."

When she realized there was nothing else to the single room, she dropped into the hard plastic of the chair and leaned her arms on the table, resting her forehead against them.

She fought a surge of self-pity that threatened to bring more tears and anger. Never in her life had she spent the night in a pit like this. Her parents and grandparents always stayed in five-star hotels and resorts. Even as a child, she had visited some of the finest hotels in the country. Her grandparents loved to travel and they always took her with them. Mostly, she missed the security she felt when Mac and Nana were near. It didn't matter what kind of hotel they stayed in, as long as they were together.

Myles snorted, but didn't wake up, and the lumps in the pillows next to his head were clearly visible from where she sat.

Would she ever return to traveling with her grandparents? Would she ever return to the life she once knew?

God, please help me to get back to my family. Back to the life I had. I just want things to be the way that they were. I miss Mac and Nana. Please just help me to get back to them.

Oh, and please take care of Myles. He's really been so good to me. And You know how much I like him. He's a good man. So please, would You mind taking care of him when I go back?

When Kenzie woke from her catnap, her eyes felt like sandpaper on the soft tissue of her eyelids. Her neck ached, and she twisted it from side to side, attempting to work out the painful kinks. Her left hand tingled, refusing to wake up.

A quick glance around the room told her that God had not instantly answered her prayers for a return to her family. Myles still snored softly on the bed next to her chair. Stale smoke had now seeped into her clothes, and she could smell it on her collar.

A loud growl echoed in the room, and she almost missed the fact that it came from her own stomach. She couldn't remember the last time they'd eaten a full meal. Probably the beef stew that Lenora had fixed for them just before they left the cabin. Even that felt like a million years ago. She was far removed from everything, from every bit of the world that could clue her in to the passing of time. Had it been a week? Two?

It couldn't be that long. Probably only a few days. Maybe four or five? She really had no clue at all. She moved to turn on the television, hoping for some news, but a sudden snort from Myles reminded her that he needed as much sleep as he could get in the next few days.

"Brammm, hmmm," he mumbled. But a small smile curved the corners of his lips, and he looked more peaceful than he had since they left the prison. However many days ago that had been.

Without thinking, she ran her fingers over his forehead and ruffled the thick brown hair at his temples. She didn't realize that she had been checking for a fever until a surge of relief flooded her. They were far from the cabin in the woods. Far from that first night after the mountain lion attack. He was fine. Would be fine. But he probably needed new pants.

I probably need new pants, too.

The glaring red stain on her own pant leg proved her theory. New pants and maybe a clean shirt. She smiled at the thought. Clean anything these days was an improvement.

The harsh light of the midday sun no longer flooded the room from the sides of the moth-eaten curtains, but it was getting close to disappearing for the rest of the night. She would have to hurry to find new clothes, food and a first-aid kit before it got dark. For the first time in her life, something in her heart told her that the night wasn't safe for her. She'd never been scared of the dark. Not even as a child.

One of her first memories was of Mac tucking her into her bed at his home. She had whimpered about the proverbial monster in the closet, and he had told her to never fear the dark. In his deep baritone he said, "A great man once said that you have nothing to fear but fear itself. You have nothing to fear here." He'd kissed her forehead and snuggled the quilt in tighter under her chin. Then he'd clicked off the bedside lamp, walked into the hallway and closed the door.

She slept very soundly that night. And every night since. Until Myles Borden slammed into her life, disrupting everything she knew and treasured.

She shot him one more glance, then hurried to the door. She turned the knob with a small click, then ever so slowly inched it open.

One leg through the doorway and the hinge creaked loudly.

"Going somewhere?"

Kenzie spun around as though caught with her hand in the cookie jar. She slammed the door shut, then leaned her back against the three locks. "Well, I'm hungry. And you need new pants and a first-aid kit."

The corner of his eyes crinkled in a smile, even if his lips didn't move. After assessing her for a few moments, he finally said, "Be careful. And be back before dark. Please." He rolled onto his left side and was snoring again instantly.

Sure her affirming nod was lost to his sleeping figure, she

hurried out the door, looking up and down the street for signs of life, stores and police officers.

It was pitch-black when Myles awoke, his head no longer spinning, but his right leg in severe pain. He tested his left knee by bending it slowly, until his foot rested flat against the bed. Pain. Maybe a six. He could handle a six.

It was the eight in the other leg that was causing his eyes to water copiously and his nose to drip. He headed toward the bathroom in search of a tissue.

Immediately, his nose connected with the wall to the left of the bed. "Yeoww!" he howled. He had to bite his tongue to keep from screaming a few choice words that had been part of his everyday vocabulary in the navy.

He cupped his hands around his nose, plunked back onto the bed and waited for the blood to pour and his head to stop spinning. After several seconds the blood still had not come, so he stood again.

The darkness consumed the room, and he suddenly remembered Kenzie. She had promised to be back before dark. Where could she be? Maybe she was sleeping? Or sitting at the table?

"Kenzie. Kenzie!" No response. She wasn't back yet.

First things first—he needed to find the light. With slow, calculated movements, he reached out to the wall and pressed his hand flat. He followed it in the direction of the foot of the bed and quickly found a corner. Turning with the wall, he found a door. The front door? A closet?

He reached through the open door with one hand and protected his nose with another. He tried to sniff the air, get a feel for his surroundings, but his nose was useless for the time being. He waved his hand around on the other side of the doorway and squinted into the blackness.

Nothing.

He felt and saw nothing. But the frontier needed to be explored. Drawing his back a little straighter, he took baby steps into the unknown, still protecting his throbbing nose.

Shortly, his knee connected with porcelain, and his hand felt a small handle. When he pushed, water rushed through the bowl, swishing around and around.

Well, at least the bathroom would have a light switch he could turn on. He groped the wall until he found the little switch and flicked on the lights. Even the soft bulb beneath a grimy globe made his eyes burn. Blinking rapidly, he slammed his hand against the switch, plunging himself into darkness again.

Ah, relief.

He sagged against the wall, then pushed himself upright and moved out of the bathroom and backtracked until he found the bed. He sat with his back against the headboard, propped against two flat pillows, legs out straight and arms crossed over his chest.

He scowled into the blackness and waited.

And waited.

Except for crossing the room to the light switch, which his body screamed was not an option, he had no way of confirming how long he sat there. The alarm clock on the bedside table was not digital and his watch, the digital, glow-in-the-dark, two-time-zone one that had been a gift from his parents when he graduated from law school, was with his FBI badge in a safe in his office. But at least it wasn't at the prison, which he'd never go back to. Not even for another assignment. Scowling, he grudgingly admitted to himself that there was only one reason he'd ever go inside the prison again.

If Kenzie needed him.

Even without an external clock, his internal timepiece told him that about thirty-five minutes passed before Kenzie returned. The minutes ticked by achingly slowly. He drummed his fingers on the rough quilt, lay down and tried to get more rest. He eyed the corner of the room where he assumed a TV sat. Then he contemplated going out after her, but the twinge in his leg warned him that was an unreasonable, ridiculous idea at this point.

And then the lock on the door clicked loudly. The wood scraped the door frame and a sliver of light fell across the hideous shag carpet and onto the corner of the bed. It reached Myles's foot, illuminating his ratty tennis shoe.

He couldn't make out Kenzie's face, shadowed by the fuzzy light outside the door to their room, but he imagined her eyes wide, seeing him sitting up in bed. When she spoke, her tone didn't disappoint.

"Myles! You're up. How are you feeling?"

She bustled across the room toward the far corner. He heard what sounded like paper crinkling, then she flicked on the floor lamp next to the table. Blinking against the light, he forced himself to continue looking at her.

A brown paper grocery bag sat on the table next to her, and she smiled brightly. "I picked us up something to eat. I'm starving!" She immediately began unloading things from the bag and chattering away. "We don't have a refrigerator or microwave, so I tried to come up with some things that don't need to be cooled or heated. And I know you need to eat to get your strength back."

She held up a bag of baby carrots and he scowled. Here she was being Sweet Kenzie, and he was in the mood to verbally spar with Spicy Kenzie.

She continued ignoring him, unloading bread, peanut butter, jelly, a bag of apples and something that looked like a short, brown can of soda. In the dim light and at this distance, he was sure he was mistaken, but he couldn't figure out what he was looking at.

"I even remembered to get utensils and plates!" She held up her purchases as trophies, dancing them back and forth in front of her.

"Great," he mumbled.

Kenzie cocked her head to one side and looked right into his face. "What's wrong?" Simple and sweet. To-the-point Kenzie.

Myles glowered and tried again to bring back Spicy. "I just thought you might like to know that I've been pacing in my mind for the last half an hour, going crazy with worry. I told you to be back before dark."

"Just in your mind? What, I don't rate actually walking?"

"Well, that hurts too much."

She threw her head back and laughed as she slipped onto the edge of the bed next to him and put her hand on his cheek. "I'm sorry I'm late. There was a police officer at the grocery store."

His hand reached up and locked around her wrist. His other hand cupped her neck and he pulled her to his chest, holding her close, making sure she was really there. He needed to confirm that she wasn't an illusion.

Obligingly, she tucked her head under his chin and just rested against him. His heart returned to its normal pace. Had it been racing? He hadn't even noticed. But now, with her in his arms, holding her close, Myles realized just how scared he had been. He ran his hand over her back one more time, just for good measure, then gripped her by her shoulders and pushed her back so he could look into her face.

"Did he see you? The cop?"

"No." She smiled. "I wasn't bothering anyone, and I kept to myself. He was too busy chatting with the pretty clerk to notice me."

"I'm glad you're okay." Heaving a deep breath, he continued. "But from here on out, we don't go anywhere without the other. Agreed?"

She nodded and quickly moved back to prepare her feast. In no time at all, she whipped together two peanut butter and jelly sandwiches and handed him a plate holding them both.

"Both for me?" he quirked an eyebrow.

"You're a growing boy and all. We've got to keep you well fed."

He chuckled, then bowed his head to say a quick prayer. Suddenly Kenzie's voice interrupted his thoughts.

"Will you pray for me, too?" she asked.

He looked up at her expectant face and nodded. "God, thanks for keeping us safe. Thanks for this food. Please be with us as we try to figure out this whole situation. In Your name, amen."

Shortly, Kenzie joined him again, sitting at the end of the bed, legs crossed, a plate with her own sandwich in front of her. She tossed him a red apple and began munching on her own.

The first sandwich was gone in three bites, and Myles licked his fingers, mumbling his appreciation. "Grape jelly. My favorite."

"Mine, too," Kenzie chuckled.

He stared at her for several long moments and finally said, "Thank you."

"For what?" she asked around a bite of sticky peanut butter.

"For risking everything just to feed us. For making me take you along." He realized for maybe the first time that he really meant it. He was so thankful not to be doing this alone. Somehow, having Kenzie along for the ride made the whole situation bearable.

"Anytime!" she chirped. She crammed the rest of her sandwich into her mouth and chewed loudly. "Nana would be so ashamed of me if she could see me now. What happened to my good table manners?"

Myles laughed. "No table. No manners required."

They finished eating their dinner in silence, filling up on baby carrots and washing it all down with murky water from the tap.

As she picked up Myles's plate and swept a few crumbs from the bedspread onto the plate, Kenzie said, "Well, are we going to call Joe?" Her eyes glanced to the old-fashioned phone on the bedside table.

"We can't call Joe from here." He was just as curious as Kenzie about the name and phone number on the slip of paper that she had found in Whitestall's guard uniform. But they had to be smart about it.

"Why not?"

He shrugged. "We have no idea what we're calling into. What if they are tracking the call? What if they are only expecting a call at a certain time and we blow it? What if they have the U.S. Marshals monitoring it? Too many what-ifs. We need a safe place to come back to, and right now that's the Jewel Motel. We can't put that in jeopardy yet. It's getting late and I'm beat. We'll call from a pay phone tomorrow."

Kenzie shrugged. "If you think that's best."

"I do."

She tossed him the item from the table that, in the dim light and from a distance, looked like a short can of soda. It landed softly into his outstretched hands. An ace bandage. She chucked a small white plastic container at him. He flipped it over and saw the large red cross on the front.

"I picked up another pair of pants for you, and we don't need those covered in blood, too. Fix yourself up."

"Oh." Not his wittiest retort, but the girl had a good point.

"Now, get some sleep. I'll be in the car if you need me."

"No, let me," he argued.

She only shook her head and slipped out the door. "It's my turn. You need the rest and the bed. I'll see you in the morning."

TWELVE

Myles's fingers drummed ceaselessly on the black steering wheel of his grandma's old sedan. His injured leg bounced in rhythm to the tapping of his hands, and his head jerked every four beats to the tempo within.

The car radio was turned off, and the only other sound in the vehicle was Kenzie's deep breaths. They sat in the car outside of an almost deserted gas station. The gas pump attendant milled around the pumps, filling up windshield washing fluids and rinsing the ground with a garden hose. But the only other car, a red, classic Volkswagen Karmann Ghia, parked in front of the small station house, was also the transportation for the man standing at the crumbling pay phone booth at the corner of the building.

The man in khaki pants and a black, short-sleeve shirt stood with his back to them, head ducked down. He just needed a baseball cap to look more conspicuously like he was hiding from something or someone.

Kenzie must have been thinking the same thing as she pulled the hat off her own head, letting her red hair fall around her shoulders. The sunglasses remained perched on her nose as she shook her hair out one more time.

"When this is all said and done, you should wear your hair

down more." Myles almost clamped his hands over his mouth. How could he say something like that?

Kenzie glanced at him out of the corner of her eye and a tiny smile tugged at the corner of her lips. "Why?"

"It…just…well—" When had he become such an ineloquent clod? He cleared his throat and tried again. "It's very fetching when it's down."

"Fetching, huh? And are you saying that you'll be around to appreciate its fetchingness—you know—when all is said and done?"

He'd backed himself into this corner. But if the punch in his gut told him anything, it was that he sure wanted to be around to appreciate it. He imagined having free rein to run his fingers through all of that fiery silk. To have her rely on him and expect him to protect her when this was all over. He wanted to be there for her, forever.

He choked aloud on his own silent thoughts. What was it about Kenzie Thorn that made his mind wander down these dangerous paths? And this thought track was definitely unsafe. No good ever came of wishing about what-ifs. And until this assignment was complete, everything about a future with Kenzie was a what-if.

He needed a new topic to think about. Now.

Trying to sidestep the conversation he had started by picking on the guy on the phone, he said, "He looks like he can afford a cell phone. Wonder why he's not using it."

Kenzie shot Myles a smirk, but let him off the hook and followed the new line in the conversation. "Probably for the same reason we wouldn't use a cell phone if we had one."

"Ah, he's on the lam, too, you think? Could be."

She pushed his shoulder and laughed. "He doesn't want to be tracked."

"So he's hiding out from the little missus?"

"No! I'll bet he's ordering a really nice gift for her and doesn't want her to find out."

"Or he's bribing a city councilman for better parking on his street," Myles mused.

"More likely, he's trying to reach his daughter who isn't talking to him and won't pick up if she sees it's him on the caller ID."

"Or…maybe he's checking in with the parole officer his wife doesn't know he has."

"Don't be deranged. He's obviously calling the police about the suspicious white sedan parked in front of a service station and not filling up with gas. Being a good citizen and all."

Myles chuckled. "Oh, of course, turning in the two felon-looking guys in the front seat of said sedan is only the proper and citizenly thing to—"

Whack! Whack! Whack!

Myles's head banged against the car's ceiling, sending sunbursts in front of his eyes. He hacked and coughed for several seconds, trying to remove his tongue from his throat. Fingernails from the passenger in the seat next to him dug unrelentingly into his right forearm.

When his eyes finally stopped watering enough for him to see who had pounded on his window, he made out a gray uniform from ankles to chin. And a name sewn above the wearer's heart: Jimmy.

Myles rolled his window down about four inches and looked hard into the face of the boy who had been hosing down the gas pumps just two minutes before.

"Do you need a fill-up, mister? I'm about to go on break, so if you need gas, I'll fill it up now or you'll have to wait twenty minutes."

Myles gave him a scowl. "We're fine," he said, putting his hand over his heart, thankful that it was returning to its normal speed. He rolled the window back up and looked at Kenzie. Lips pulled tightly and eyes crinkled at the corner, she looked ready to explode. Snorting once, then again, she swallowed deeply and sighed.

"I thought we were toast, but the look of sheer panic on your face would have kept me laughing all the way back to Mac and Nana's."

"Well, I appreciate your concern," he deadpanned, "but I would be going back to the big house for quite a while. No cause for mirth there."

"No, I suppose not." She sighed again, closed her eyes and laid her hand on his arm.

"But of course, we have to live in a state where a man can't pump his own gas," he growled. "If it weren't for that crazy kid, my heart rate would be normal instead of through the top of my head."

"Oh, you poor thing. You know, we could always go to another pay phone."

"No, this one is perfect." And it was. Pay phones were hard to come by these days. With every kid and his little brother getting a cell phone on a family plan, pay phones had gone the way of the dodo. To find a phone seventeen blocks from the Jewel Motel was nothing short of ideal. Five blocks west. Six north. Six more west. Not too close—no less than two other motels on the route between the two locations. Not too far—a walkable distance if necessary.

Ideal.

After all, once they placed a call from this location, they would either be tracked or—Myles hoped—ignored. Either way, this phone would not give away their location.

Just then Mr. Bribing-his-daughter-for-a-special-gift-for-his-wife walked away from the phone. He hopped into his little coupe and zipped out of the parking lot.

"Well, kid, this is it." Myles produced the scrap of yellow paper from his pocket and held it with his fingertips. "If a cop shows up, don't worry about me—just get out of here. Okay?"

Kenzie nodded and he turned to get out of the car. Suddenly she grabbed his arm. "Get a newspaper while you're out there. Please." It was his turn to nod, then he hopped out of the car and stalked toward the deserted pay phone.

God, please let there be something to help us at the other end of this phone number. He plunked a dime and quarter from his pocket and listened to them roll down the slot, clinking as they hit the bottom. He punched in the ten digits onto the sticky number pad and waited as the phone on the other end rang twice.

His stomach bunched in knots, his hands clammy, Myles took a deep breath. No amount of training prepared anyone for an unknown phone call that could either make or break a case.

The phone on the other end stopped ringing; someone took a deep breath and in a gravelly voice said, "Larry? Where have you been? No one's seen hide nor hair of you in days!"

Myles grunted, not sure how to answer.

"Joe" grumbled something unsavory, but continued on. "It doesn't matter. It's probably better anyway! So get on with it. Have you heard from the inmate? Well? Is she dead?"

Kenzie sat in the passenger seat of her car as she watched Myles step up to the phone booth next to the front entrance of the small building. He picked up the phone, dialed the number and then ruffled his hair impatiently. Sunlight glinted off the metal partitions jutting out from the wall. A gust of wind kicked a white plastic bag along the ground and then spun it around several times. The theme from the old television show *Gunsmoke* whistled through her head, as Kenzie imagined the bag to be tumbleweed.

She supposed that her situation could be considered something like an old Western. There was definitely a bad guy, and certainly Myles could be construed as a modern-day cowboy in his jeans and cotton T-shirt, his rakish brown hair blowing gently in the breeze. Likely at least several of the players in this Western owned cowboy hats—and in small-town Oregon, they probably owned horses, too.

A grin quirked the corner of her mouth as she let her mind wander to a place where she and Myles rode horses through open pastures, galloping away from the men in black hats who chased them. Suddenly one of the men in black pulled a gun and fired it at them.

Crack!

Even though it was imagined, the sound of the gunfire shook Kenzie from her trance. It also opened up a whole new realm of possibilities in the real world. She could not be sure why it had never occurred to her until now, but the men chasing her and Myles were armed, were dangerous—likely wouldn't hesitate before shooting Myles.

A knot settled in the bottom of Kenzie's stomach, and she pondered it for several seconds. Although she expected it to be a nervous response to the feeling of being watched—likely by the men in black hats—a quick glance around the parking lot told her they were more or less alone. The fill-up kid slouched along the side of the building, chugging back what appeared to be an energy drink. No other cars had pulled into the station while she daydreamed.

But the knot remained. Was it just fear for Myles? She sorted through her thoughts as methodically as possible, hunting for the root of the tension. Myles stood with his back to her, his shoulders wide, stable. Feet planted shoulder-width apart looked as though an earthquake would not move them. His hand combed through this hair, and he swung the offending strands from his forehead with a quick toss of his head, completely nonchalant and on the phone with their one chance at cracking open this entire nightmare.

No, she wasn't afraid for Myles. He could take care of himself. Kenzie grudgingly admitted to herself that she had been letting him take care of her for the last— Well, for as long as they'd been on the run. Even if she took care of his injuries, she thrived on his stability. Nothing rattled him, and she clung to that core of power that he radiated.

Myles could take care of the both of them.

So why was her stomach tied so tight?

When the knot first arrived, she had been thinking of riding horses, and Myles and the bad guys chasing them and…

The bad guys chasing them?

Kenzie let her head fall into her hands. Head pounding, she fought to isolate the gut feeling that said something was wrong.

And then it was there, so glaring, so obvious. Why hadn't she thought about this before?

Where were the men that Mac had surely hired to track her down? Why weren't there roadblocks and police searches going on all over? There were no wanted posters plastered in store windows. No notices tacked to phone poles promising money for her safe return. There had been only that one news-paper article offering a reward.

She and Myles had tried to be careful—always paying with the cash from the cabin, not visiting major chain stores or gas stations that would have video cameras—but certainly they were having better-than-average luck.

Brows furrowed, she glanced up just in time to see a blue-and-red reflection glinting off the metal partition next to Myles's shoulder. He obviously saw the same thing, because he spun on the spot and made a frantic swiping motion with his left arm and slammed the phone down at the same time.

From this distance, she could almost read his lips yelling, "It's a cop!"

Kenzie hurdled the dividing console and fell into the driver's seat, cranking the engine to life without a second thought. Jamming the gear shift into Reverse, she plowed through the gas station parking lot. Two plastic trash cans filled with windshield cleaner sailed through the air, and a gray cement barrier jumped out of nowhere. Her front bumper left a six-inch white kiss on it as she hurtled onto the almost-deserted street.

In her rearview mirror Myles dashed through the open parking lot and into an alley between two deserted, gray cinder block buildings. The police car swerved to follow her, but then thought better and chased after Myles. The black-and-white burned rubber as it plowed toward the narrow alley.

"I've got to get Myles!" she wailed to the empty car. "But how?"

She slammed on her brakes to avoid the car that suddenly appeared in front of her. Cranking the wheel to her right, she skidded through the turn onto a side street with an unfamiliar name. Rolling down the window and straining for the sound of sirens, she sailed in the direction she thought Myles was headed. He would not lead the police officer to the motel, but neither would he go in the completely opposite direction.

Myles had told her to save herself if the police showed up. Even though she had agreed to it, she knew the truth. She couldn't leave him behind. They were in this together.

Swerving around two large metal dumpsters lining the one-way street, Kenzie floored the accelerator, one eye on the road in front of her and one on her rearview mirror. Backup was likely very close, but she could still hear nothing over the sound of her own engine and the wild thumping of her heart in her ears.

And then a flash of blue and green sprinted across the street several blocks in front of her. It looked like blue jeans and a green T-shirt. If she squinted—Myles?

A black-and-white police car sailed across the same intersection.

Myles!

Almost ripping the steering wheel from its base, Kenzie turned the car one block in front of Myles and the police car, flying down the narrow alley. She caught a glimpse of the police car's rear bumper at the next intersection and continued down her own alley, bumping into a Dumpster.

A man carrying a garbage bag flung open a screen door just after the next Dumpster. Laying on the horn, Kenzie kept her path. He jumped back just in time, landing on his backside, clutching the large bag of trash. He raised a shaking fist and opened his mouth to yell at her, but she was far past the point of hearing or caring.

She absolutely had to find Myles. They were in this mess together, and without him she had no one to trust. Would Mac or Nana or anyone else believe her if she tried to explain all that had happened in just a few short days? Highly unlikely. Would it ever be safe to return to the prison, to the prisoners she loved teaching? Her only chance seemed to lie with Myles.

Myles, who was injured and running flat-out from a police cruiser. He couldn't keep this up for long.

But Myles was smart. If he couldn't outrun the cruiser, what would he do?

Kenzie slammed on her brakes and skidded to a stop right at the mouth of the next intersection. The black-and-white soared through the intersection one block down, its lights flashing, but no sirens blaring. Kenzie waited for ten seconds, then slowly pulled into normal traffic. One block down, she turned to retrace the path of the cruiser, hoping beyond reason to find Myles stashed somewhere, lurking in a doorway, or hiding beside a Dumpster.

She was creeping along the empty road and peering into every doorway and recess, when…

Thud!

The enormous jolt stole her breath. And the man's seemingly lifeless body on the hood of her car stopped her heart.

THIRTEEN

"Myles Borden!" Kenzie screeched, yanking at Myles's feet as he slid off the hood of the car. Kenzie stood with her hands on her hips next to the open car door and glared at him. He just walked around her and slid into the driver's seat, his laughter only fueling her irritation. She had no choice but to hurry to the other side of the car and jump in. "What if I had really hit you?" she demanded as he drove them back in the direction of the gas station.

"Well, you didn't."

Being forced to physically restrain herself from hitting him made the next words shoot out of her mouth. "But I could have! You're a jerk for letting me think I had hurt you."

His head tilted to the left and he rumbled, "Forget about it."

"I will not! How could you be so mean to me?"

"I didn't mean to be make you so upset."

"But you're all that I have right now!" She couldn't refrain from the exclamations as they exploded from somewhere near the pit of her stomach. "What would happen if I didn't have you? What would I do?" The fear making her voice shake shamed her to the core, and she hated the truth it revealed. Without him she was lost.

"So now this is all about you?"

"What?"

His lips twitched and it seemed to take him some effort to force them back into a straight line. "Well, it's just that every statement you just made was about you."

"That's not true."

"It is, too," he said.

She huffed and crossed her arms over her chest. The man was incorrigible.

"Don't worry. I'm really okay, so you won't be alone yet or anything." His lips quirked and he rubbed his left knee. With the other hand he patted his right leg. "I didn't even reopen the scratch on my leg."

"And now it's a scratch? You mean that little cut that's been either profusely bleeding or making you lose consciousness for the last…I don't know how many days!" How dare he belittle such an important thing!

Suddenly, the rough pads of his fingers lay gently on her wrist, massaging the skin right above her pulse. She wanted to yank her arm away. To leave him feeling as deserted as she had. To give him a void that he couldn't fill.

To leave her arm just out of reach of his for eternity.

Her initial instinct won out, and she pulled away, squinting at him under pinched brows. Her forehead ached from the force of pulling her eyebrows together so tightly, but he deserved to know that acting this way would not be tolerated.

"Kenzie, I'm okay. Don't worry." He gestured to his right leg. "The leg feels good. The knee isn't going to fall off. We're both fine. The cops are none the wiser."

"How can you say that? They were chasing you. And in two minutes backup would have been chasing you, too." Myles snorted, but she forged ahead. "Don't you see? Your shenanigans put us in serious trouble."

"My shenanigans? *My* shenanigans? Whoa, back that bus up. When did this all turn into *my* fault?"

"It's always been your fault!"

"Since when? I think if this is anyone's fault, it's most likely yours."

She wanted to blame him, to thrust the blame for this entire horrible situation on someone else. The truth hurt, and she fought with her heart over accepting it.

Finally, her shoulders drooped and she said, "You're right."

"I am?" The surprise clear in his voice, Myles nearly swerved the car into a curb.

"Yes." She couldn't offer him anything else just yet. Accepting that the danger they faced was her fault took some getting used to. Attempting to change the topic of conversation, she asked, "Where are we going?"

"We're going to ditch the car in the alley by the gas station."

"Why? Won't we have to walk back to the motel?"

"Yep. No two ways about that. That cop made this car, and it won't be long before they figure out it was you and me in it. We've got to get rid of the car."

"But the cruiser was chasing you."

"Yes, but the cop definitely saw this car, and even the least adept cop won't miss the scratch on the bumper that matched the kiss you gave that barrier in the parking lot."

"You saw that?" Heat rose in her neck and cheeks and she refused to look at him.

Myles chuckled. "Couldn't miss it. It's no big deal, but we've got to get rid of the car, and we need to do it close to the place where we were originally spotted. Whether they've made us out as who we really are remains to be seen. But the fact is that the cops will be looking for me and for this car. So we'll ditch the car, and then we'll have to wait until night to make our way back to the motel."

Pulling into the alley adjacent to the station, Myles slipped the keys out of the ignition and pushed them into the pocket of his jeans. Using the hem of his T-shirt, he rubbed off the steering wheel, window crank and radio dials. "Do your door handle, too." She followed suit, and soon the inside of the car was devoid of any distinguishable prints. He jerked his head toward his door and said, "Let's go."

Kenzie slid from the car and hurried to catch up with Myles's long strides, leading deeper into the alley. About halfway down the next street, Myles slipped between two six-foot metal Dumpsters. He pushed the one farther from the car about a foot from the cement wall and proceeded to wedge himself into the tight spot.

"You coming?"

"Yes," she mumbled, slipping into place beside him. The harsh texture of the cement wall on her back contrasted with the gentle-as-a-breeze brush of his knuckles across the back of her hand. Her stomach fluttered madly, and her head quickly followed suit. Disgusted with her immediate reaction to the gentlest touch from Myles, she blew wayward strands of hair off her cheeks with jagged puffs. Sweat trickled down the back of her neck.

She eyed the setting sun appreciatively. Soon the darkness would bring cooler temperatures, and the humidity would be less oppressive. And with any luck, the rotting refuse in the garbage bins would reek less.

A girl could dream.

Suddenly Myles's voice broke into her daydream of trash that smelled of roses. "Aren't you going to ask me about the phone call?"

"Oh, my—" she squeaked. "I forgot! What happened? Did someone pick up the phone? What did they say?"

"Easy there, Lois Lane. You're not on deadline for your story, are you?"

"Just tell me what happened," she begged.

"A man answered the phone. He had a thick, gravelly—"

"What?"

"Sshhh." If there had been room to maneuver, Myles would have put his finger to his lips. Instead he whispered, "Someone's coming."

Kenzie breathed heavily beside him, tension evident in every jagged inhale. A crow squawked at the far end of the alley. The sun slipped behind the mountains, sending shadows away for the night.

Crunch.

A heavy foot fell on the loose gravel at the narrow mouth of the passageway near their abandoned car. Kenzie grabbed Myles's hand and squeezed his fingers until he had no feeling there, but she remained silent, save her shaky breathing.

"Davis!" a man's voice hollered. "Get over here! I think I found the car."

A second set of footfalls joined the first, these lighter, more graceful. A woman's voice joined the man's. "Looks like you're right. See that gash on the front bumper? It matches the mark on the barrier in the gas station. You really think it was Myles Parsons?"

"The man we were chasing matches the description of Parsons perfectly. I can't believe our luck to pull alongside an escaped convict and then give chase. I don't think I would have recognized him if he hadn't taken off running."

Myles cringed. But it was too late to take back the chase now. He'd done what he thought he needed to to protect Kenzie.

"Too bad he got away," the woman mocked.

The sound of tape ripping off of metal reached Myles in his hiding place. They were looking for fingerprints.

"Do you think the governor's granddaughter is still with him? And what are they doing in Evergreen? Shouldn't Parsons be in Canada by now? Why would he stick around here?" Davis said.

"Maybe he's stashing the girl's body in the woods..." Kenzie gasped loudly at the same moment that a bird screeched and Myles offered up a silent prayer of thanksgiving for crazy birds "...and came into town for supplies or to meet up with an accomplice, which accounts for the one driving the car while I chased Parsons on foot."

"Well, we better call the U.S. Marshals on this. They're after Parsons and will never forgive us if we don't call them in right away." The heavier steps walked away, while the lighter footfalls circled the car several times. Finally, the woman seemed to follow her partner.

"How long do we have to stay here?" Kenzie breathed.

"A while longer," Myles answered equally as soft.

Kenzie sighed and rested her head on the green cotton covering his shoulder, her hand still holding his, much more gently than before. It was almost dark enough to make a dash for it. But he couldn't risk it with police so near. They would wait here as long as they needed.

Kenzie couldn't help the smile that tugged at the corners of her lips as she snuggled close to Myles. The stars above reminded her of the twinkling lights from her high school prom so many years before. Tonight there were no starched tuxedo shirts, but the cotton of Myles's secondhand shirt was soft as a baby's skin. Crammed between a trash Dumpster and a rough wall definitely was not the Radisson, and there would be no swaying to love songs, but the solid muscular shoulder under her cheek was the most perfect feeling in the world.

His breath ruffled the hair on top of her head, and she

leaned into him just a little closer. For a moment a breeze lifted Myles's scent to her nose, and she relished his musky aroma and the relief from the odor of rotting garbage.

Clouds danced in front of the moon, pitching the alley into almost complete darkness. The two police officers seemed set on inspecting every inch around the car, and their voices still carried, if somewhat indistinguishable.

"See anything?" the man asked.

"No. It's getting too dark, and the batteries in my flash-light died."

"I've got some extras in the trunk. Be right back."

Both cops moved farther away, and Myles breathed, "Get ready. When the next cloud covers the moon. Stay light on your feet. Hold my hand, and don't let go. Whatever happens, we stick together."

Kenzie squeezed his hand in response and watched a lone cloud float toward the white orb. And then it was covered, and Myles tugged on her hand, pulling her toward the far end of the Dumpster and the open alley.

Scraping along the cement, her back arched away from the pain, and she shuffled as silently as possible. They broke into the open air, free of the oppressive odor that made her eyes water and exposed for the entire world to see. Myles's feet hit silently on the ground as he ran in front of her, his left hand holding her right one in a vise grip.

She strained for any sound near their abandoned car, but all was silent except for the echoing of her canvas shoes hitting the gravel with each step. The sound exploded in her head, bouncing from ear to ear, certainly alerting the cops to their presence.

But Myles kept running, and no noise came from the other end of the alley. A stitch in her side tried to stop her, but Kenzie kept flying after Myles's silhouette, his hand holding hers a calming force. Heart beating double time, she saw the end of the alley. Fifty feet to go…twenty-five.

"Hey! Who's there?" A single light beam flashed across Myles's back, but he never stopped running. In four seconds they were around the corner, running at top speed down a smooth sidewalk. The change in surface was both strange and welcome.

Heavy steps fell in the gravel, just around the corner behind them.

"In here." Myles heaved, yanking Kenzie into a doorway to a run-down motel. He tore open the door and said, "Got a bathroom for the lady?" His head jerked in her direction.

The girl behind the counter couldn't have been much out of high school. She popped a large bubble of gum and mumbled, "It's for paying customers."

Myles dug a twenty of out his pocket and tossed it at the girl, who pointed down the dingy hallway. The flickering light halfway down the hall exposed the peeling wallpaper and matted carpet.

When they were out of earshot, Kenzie whispered, "You don't really expect me to use this bathroom, do you?"

Myles didn't bother to answer her, he just pushed her past the door marked "Women" and followed her into the tiny room, closing and locking the door behind them both. Apparently the answer to her question was negative.

The bathroom was as disgusting as she had expected, given the state of the rest of the building. Rust stains littered the linoleum floor next to the base of the toilet. Cracks in the wall at the baseboards looked like the perfect place for mice and other unspeakable creatures to sneak in and out of. A tiny speck of white on the sink next to the faucet showed what color the entire counter had once been. It likely hadn't been that color in years. Even more likely, it hadn't seen a sponge in almost as long.

A small brown cockroach crawled up from the drain, causing Kenzie to shriek. "Can we get out of here?" she whined, nodding toward the creepy bug. Myles followed her line of vision and cringed.

"I'm on it," he said, and followed with quick action. He slammed the lid down on the toilet seat and quickly stood on it. Lifting the tiny window above the tank with one hand, he reached out with the other. "Come on." He pulled her to his side and then quickly swept her up into his arms, like she weighed nothing.

Suddenly the door handle jiggled.

Then again, this time with some force. A hip or a shoulder crashed into the decaying wood. Any minute the police would be in the tiny room with them, but all she could think about was the curve of Myles's lips and the deep blue of his eyes.

On the run from the police and in the most disgusting bathroom she had ever seen, this was the wrong place and the worst time. But in the split second that Myles held her to his chest, she knew that she could not pass up this opportunity. By sleeping in the car, by protecting her, caring for her, he had more than earned a repeat of that toe-curling kiss he'd given her for her birthday. Had it really only been two days before?

Who cared that this wasn't the perfect time or place? It would have to do. And when she focused on the blue of his eyes, the crook of his nose, and the pink of his lips, the rest of the room disappeared. Wrapping her arms around his neck, she leaned in until she was just inches from his lips. "Thank you."

"For what?" His voice was hoarse and loaded with emotion. He bumped the brim of her cap up higher, out of his way.

The door handle jiggled violently again, and a body slammed once more into the door, accompanied by a loud grunt.

"For everything." She smiled, cutting the distance between their lips in half. "For kidnapping me. For saving me. For protecting me. For being so honor—"

Her words cut off as he pressed his lips against hers, crushing her to his chest with his arms. His lips were gentle and tender in contrast to the strength of his embrace. And she couldn't help but smile at the way her heart pounded against his, as if dueling for the title of most affected.

He pulled back after a moment, then leaned in once more for a swift, more urgent connection. He gently ripped his lips from hers, a rakish grin spread from ear to ear. "You pick the worst, least romantic time and place to kiss me? What kind of woman are you?"

She could hear the teasing in his voice, but it didn't stop the flush of embarrassment that worked its way up her neck. Nana would be scandalized by her actions. Perhaps that's why Nana did not need to know about this particular event.

"Just a moment please!" Myles called to the growing disturbance on the other side of the door.

Kenzie cleared her throat. "I—I couldn't help myself."

Myles roared with laughter. Well, she was sure he would have if he weren't trying to keep his voice low. It came out as a hoarse chortle instead, but was no less appealing. "Nice excuse. Keep it up, and we might be in big trouble if we're both using it." He gave her another peck on the lips, then slipped her feet through the open window. "No more time now." His eyes darted to the rotting door. "Stay against the building and walk to your left. I'm right behind you."

She did as he said, slipping down the wall and holding herself flat against the back wall. Her eyes darted around the side street, but she saw no police cars, no police officers, no one.

Myles's feet stuck through the window, and in one fluid motion, he swung from the window frame and dropped to his feet beside her. He winced when he hit the ground, but made no further comment. When he grabbed her hand, she asked, "Your knee or the scratch?"

He chuckled. "Both."

Then he tugged her hand and led her down the street. At the corner, he stuck his head around the building, looking for signs of their pursuers. Nothing gave him cause for concern, as he pulled her onto the street, and they walked quickly— but not fast enough to draw undue attention—toward their motel. Myles steered them out of the beams from the street-lights above.

Two blocks later he let go of her hand. "I forgot. You're still in disguise." He smiled at her, but it wasn't enough to fill the sense of loss from losing his touch.

The blocks zoomed by. Several dark-colored cars passed them, but seemed completely oblivious to their existence. And in short order they were back at the Jewel.

"I'll pay for another night," Kenzie said. She slipped into the front office, passed two bills to the clerk, mumbled something about keeping the same room in the deepest voice she could muster. Pulling her hat a little lower over her eyes, she headed back to room number three.

Inside the room Myles lay sprawled out on the bed on top of the muted brown bedspread. "I think I was more tired than I realized," he mumbled. "But I have something for you." Rolling to his side, he pulled something gray out of the back waistband of his jeans and tossed it to her.

She caught the newspaper and smiled. "We've been chased by police twice, and you still managed to get me a newspaper?"

"What can I say? You asked for it. I got it." His lips quirked as he closed his eyes again.

Kenzie sat down at the little table and immediately began shuffling through *The Oregonian*. The state's major newspaper might not be reporting about the everyday happenings in Evergreen, but it would certainly report on the governor. And maybe the governor's granddaughter.

Nothing on page one. Or two. And then on page three—the state news page—the headline: PRISON EDUCATION REFORM EXPANDS.

Just two years after being passed, the Oregon State Prison Education Reform Bill moves onto its next stage this month, more than a year ahead of schedule. The Oregon State Penitentiary and Shutter Creek Correctional Institution are both scheduled to begin GED preparation courses for inmates.

These courses will be modeled after the program at the Evergreen complex, which succeeded in passing more than two hundred inmates through the program in the past two years. The original program boasted a GED exam pass rate of nearly sixty-five percent, due in part to the lavish budget.

As stipulated in the reform bill, after two hundred inmates complete the GED preparation program, the program will be adopted at other state prisons.

Gubernatorial candidate and Circuit Court Judge Claudia Suarez supports the program, but continues to be outspoken regarding the amount of money being spent. "Education is an important part of prisoner rehabilitation," says Suarez. "I take that very seriously. But educational dollars are being spent on prisoners that should be spent in our elementary and high schools."

Governor Mackenzie Thorn could not be reached for comment. According to a spokesperson, he is grieving the kidnapping of his still-missing granddaughter, with whom he shares a name. Ms. Thorn was kidnapped five days ago by a prison inmate after she completed her day of teaching the GED preparation courses at the complex at Evergreen.

Myles snorted and flopped to his side. His eyes opened slowly, and he rubbed them with one large hand. "How long have I been out?"

"Just a few minutes."

"Anything interesting in the paper?"

"Yeah. I think so."

Myles scooted to a seated position, leaning against the headboard. "What's up? More reward money for your safe return? Money for my capture?"

"No, nothing like that. It's just an article about the prison education reform. It talks about the lavish budget for prison education, but we didn't have a big budget. I mean, I had to make homemade posters. You remember them—on the walls of my classroom?"

"That is strange." Myles stood up and read the article over her shoulder. "Where's all that money going, if it's not going to the teacher or the classroom?"

"There shouldn't be much overhead to the program. Just books and supplies and my salary. We meet at the prison— no cost there. The inmates walked to class—at no cost. No air-conditioning in the summer—no cost."

Myles rolled his shoulders and wrinkled his forehead. "I think this might tie in with my phone call today."

How could she forget about the phone call that started their crazy day? "What happened?"

Myles plopped back on the bed. "A guy on the other end of the line picked up and immediately asked if she was dead."

"'She' being me?" Kenzie couldn't contain the violent shudder of her entire body.

"I assume so. He never spoke your name. I didn't want to lie, but I couldn't exactly tell the truth, either. I just told him, 'not yet.' And he said, 'You know, it's your job to make sure that Parsons'—being me of course—'does his job. We can't disappoint Macky, now, can we?'"

Kenzie's neck snapped up from looking at the newspaper so fast that it cracked. "*What* did you say?"

"He said we don't want to disappoint Mac."

"No, you said 'Macky.' Then you said, 'Mac.' Which did he say?"

Myles furrowed his brow even deeper. "The first."

"Only one person calls my grandfather 'Macky.'"

FOURTEEN

"What?"

If Kenzie could spit fire, the entire hotel room would have been toast. She glared at Myles as if he had caused the man on the other end of the line to confess his identity.

"Whoa, there!" Myles held up his hands as if to ward off her attack. "I didn't do anything. Why are you looking at me like that?"

"Macky! Macky! That—that— What a horrid, horrid man!" she shrieked, alternately wringing and clenching her hands and marching in place. Her mind raced to call him every awful name in the book, and she might have if her tongue had cooperated. But then Myles appeared in front of her, holding her hands gently, his face a mask of concern.

"Calm down, Kenz. Tell me what's happening."

"It's Superintendent Ryker."

"What about Ryker?"

She huffed and barely refrained from yelling at him. "JB Ryker is the only man in the world who calls Mac 'Macky.' Mac wouldn't ever allow anyone else. But he and Ryker have been friends forever. *Friends!* Imagine that! Mac's *best friend* tried to have me killed!"

Understanding lit Myles's features like a morning sunrise

over the mountains, the rays tentative at first, then illuminating every crack and crevice. "Ryker? Ryker is behind this all?"

"Of course! Don't you see?"

"What does JB stand for?"

Kenzie rummaged through ancient mental files, searching for that information. "Joseph something, I think."

"Joe. I sure called Joe, didn't I?" He shook his head, mumbling to himself. "This is getting out of hand. We've got to get you into protective custody at the safe house."

"No. Not yet."

Myles began pacing the tiny room from the bed to the wall. Then from the table to the door. He made a square in the carpet and walked it over and over. His fingers tunneled through his hair and yanked wildly, as though trying to pull out every strand. He growled. "But what if it goes higher than Ryker?"

"How could it?"

"I'm not sure, but something feels off. What's in it for Ryker? What possible motive can he have for wanting you out of the way?"

Good question. Even better, she knew the answer.

"Myles, it's all here in the newspaper article. It explains everything."

He leaned over the newspaper, still open on the little table. The single floor lamp illuminated just enough space for them to read it again. The muscles of his arms bunched and flexed beneath his lightweight shirt as he leaned over the paper.

"I'm not sure that I follow," he mumbled after finishing the article for the second time and noticing the large full-color ad paid for by Mac's campaign fund.

Kenzie sighed, emotionally drained and suddenly physically exhausted. She sank to the corner of the bed and rested her knees on her elbows. "This is about the money. It's always about money. That article says that the education reform has a lavish budget. That's some pretty awful reporting, if it's incorrect. Besides, Claudia Suarez backs up that statement, saying that too much money is being spent on the prison education system.

"Like I said before, there is very little overhead for prison education. And the budget I was given by JB is anything but lavish. Somewhere between the state budget and the prison budget, money is disappearing. And I'd bet my right hand it's ending up in the superintendant's pocket."

Myles nodded, not looking completely convinced. He crossed his arms over his chest and rested against the edge of the round table. "But how does your kidnapping and murder fit into that plan? How does removing you from the situation help Ryker? Were you close to discovering any of this back at the prison?"

She shook her head slowly. "No. I had no idea that there should have been more money for the program. But maybe… I guess I could have been closer to it than I thought."

"Did Ryker ever say anything to you about the budget? Did he ever try to feel you out, to see what you might know about it?"

"Not exactly."

Myles scrubbed his face with open palms and scowled. "What exactly did he say to you?"

"Well, both years he gave me a copy of my budget for supplies, notebooks, workbooks, stuff like that. And he always reminded me that it was highly confidential information. He never came right out and threatened me, but I always got the impression that if I spilled any of the information that even my connection to Mac wouldn't be enough to keep my job."

Saying it aloud now made Kenzie cringe. How had she never realized what a dangerous man JB could be?

"I don't see it. I just don't see how that's enough to make

him want you dead." He shook his head and slouched lower, his shoulders sinking under the weight of the world.

Kenzie rubbed her chin. "A couple weeks ago, I told JB that I was going to petition the state legislature for more money in next year's budget. And I brought it up again when Mac came to visit the prison. Do you think he was worried that I would figure it out?"

"Could be. But what did he mean about not disappointing Mac?"

"Mac's not a fool. He wouldn't expect me to be returned alive, especially if there was no ransom note. He's probably already grieving with Nana, preparing her for what he assumes the police will find."

There, that was logical. Myles could argue all he wanted and look as dubious as ever, but the truth was evident. JB Ryker had tried to have her killed, and they had to focus on getting him arrested.

"We know that JB is behind this," Kenzie said. "Aren't you going to call up your supervisor and have him arrested?"

"I will, but we also need some proof."

"What kind of proof?"

Myles's lips pursed to the side. "A copy of the budget Ryker gave you, to start with. Not the official one, but the doctored budget to reflect the smaller allowance to the program."

"Fine. I can get that."

Eyebrows shooting almost to his hairline, he asked, "How do you plan to do that?"

"I'll go back to my classroom at the prison, of course."

"Over my dead body!" His face turned beet-red, and she could almost see the steam billowing out of his ears.

"How else do you plan to get the information we need? I can get the prison budget from my desk, and I'll just ask Mac for a copy of the state budget."

Myles growled again, this time low in his throat, almost from his chest. "We'll send someone from the bureau in to get your budget. There's no need for you to go back."

"Why shouldn't I go back?" Knowing she had him beat again, Kenzie smiled. "I'll steer clear of JB and make sure I stick close to someone else so I'm never alone."

He shook his head and began pacing again. "And how do you plan to return to the prison? Are you just going to waltz in after being gone for over a week? Won't they ask some questions?"

She shrugged. "I'll have to start in Salem. I'll start with Mac."

"And what are you going to say?"

"I don't know." And she really didn't have a clue. "We'll figure it out on the trip tomorrow."

"I'm not sending you back into that prison."

Kenzie just shot him the same smile that had been winning arguments since their prison break.

The Greyhound bus rocked slightly as the round driver walked up the steps and slipped behind the huge steering wheel. The engine roared to life, rattling every inch of the monster. With a loud swoosh the airbrakes released, and they began their journey toward Salem.

Myles looked down at the bill of the baseball cap covering Kenzie's face. She slouched low in the uncomfortable gray seat and remained silent for the first time in twenty-four hours. Well, that was a slight exaggeration. But the silence was a welcome relief.

Minutes ticked by slowly into half hours, then hours. The high desert landscape zipped along outside the windows, slowly changing to a more lush, green setting. But each time he checked his watch, it was only one minute later than the last time, and they were still miles from where they needed to be. Miles from the place where they would finally be able to put everything to rest.

The nearly deserted Greyhound was relatively quiet, in as much as the only other passengers were at least three rows ahead or behind them on both sides of the aisle. A man across the aisle and about four rows ahead of them seemed to be having an animated conversation with his seatmate, but his voice did not carry to them.

Myles had carefully, yet surreptitiously, surveyed all fourteen of the other passengers when they boarded the bus. And assuming that his law enforcement senses were not dulled by weeks of undercover work, injury or the crazy woman beside him, he felt certain that no one was a threat to Kenzie or him. The single mom holding her baby sat three rows ahead of them. Two teenagers sat in the very back row, most likely enjoying the privacy that location afforded.

But Myles picked the best seat on the bus. Perfect vantage point of the front door and the large mirror in front of the driver's seat. The row with the emergency window, in case they needed to make a fast break.

If only it were more comfortable. But nothing could be done about the horrid seats on the bus. The built-in lumbar support always hit him in the wrong part of the back, making it impossible to sleep through long trips.

At that moment, the only comfortable thing about the trip was the feel of Kenzie's slender shoulder leaning into his arm. Her chin tucked into her chest and her face hidden by the ball cap, he could only appreciate the unseen things about her. She smelled like earth and rain and a touch of lingering citrus—not overly flowery like so many women. An indefinable strength flowed through her shoulder and into his arm. The same strength that persuaded him time and again to do things he should have refused her.

He should have left her at the safe house. He should have stopped himself from kissing her. He should have told her they needed to wait before going to Salem.

So many should haves.

Yet somehow, he just could not say no when she dug her heels in. It was that strength that warmed his arm now.

You must have been a terror as a child, he thought. *I almost feel sorry for Mac and your grandma. What on earth did you put them through? I bet you were just smart enough to get out of every scrape that you got into. And I bet all you had to do was bat those big gray eyes at Mac and he crumbled.*

But why isn't he crumbling now? Where has he been while you've been in imminent danger for over a week? How could anyone who loves you not come to your rescue immediately? How could anyone not love you, my Sweet and Spicy Kenzie?

Sadly, he knew the truth. His phone call to Nate before they left the hotel had clarified just what he feared. Mac was involved in the conspiracy surrounding Kenzie's kidnapping.

Myles was good at analyzing clues, and he knew without a doubt that all of them pointed toward Mac's involvement in the case. It was all about the prison's education budget, which, according to the newspapers, was bulging. But Myles knew the governor had been in that classroom. Kenzie had confirmed it. There was no money there, and her grandfather knew it, despite the budget he had approved. And Myles was sure the missing money was lining the pockets of Mac *and* Ryker. Afterall, Mac's campaign fund was surprisingly healthy, if the number of ads he was running was any indication. He wasn't independently wealthy like Claudia Suarez. The money had to be coming from somewhere.

And even though Kenzie had been reading the same newspapers and collecting the same evidence, she'd seen only Ryker's involvement because she didn't want to see Mac's hand in it all. She had an understandable blind spot for her grandfather.

Nate, on the other hand, had no problem telling Myles that his hunch was correct. The tip that had originally sent Myles to prison to protect Kenzie had also included information on a connection between Mac and extra income. Now they just needed the hard evidence. Wire taps and financial records.

Myles had been happy to prove to Kenzie that he was an FBI agent. But he knew he wouldn't relish revealing whatever proof he found about Mac's involvement.

Without thinking about the action, he reached his hand up and cupped her cheek, letting his thumb brush her earlobe. She sighed and leaned a little bit closer, resting her other cheek against his shoulder.

"Whaa…" she mumbled.

"Hm?"

"What are you thinking?" she asked, forced to raise her voice over the racket of the rambling bus.

That I never should have let you talk me into this. That this is lunacy. That you're missing a big part of this picture. That we're moving prematurely. That all evidence points to Mac.

She elbowed him in the bicep. "Seriously. What are you thinking about?"

He quickly confirmed that the surrounding seats remained empty. "Just wondering how this all started. How did you end up teaching at the prison?"

She kept her face forward, but he thought he could see the corner of her mouth raised in a half smile. "I always wanted to be a teacher. It just seemed like the best profession in the world to a grade schooler who had always loved her own teachers. And by the time I got to high school, I knew it was the only thing that would make me happy.

"I also love to travel, so I figured that with a degree I could move anywhere and always be able to find a job."

"Did you ever think about teaching at any of those international programs where you teach English?"

"Not just thought about it. I went for it."

Rightfully impressed, Myles nodded his approval. "Where did you go?"

"Right after graduation, I moved to Belgium and taught English at a Bible institute there. Mac and Nana were very supportive. When I first started thinking about it during my last year in college, I was afraid that they'd try to hold me back, try to keep me close. They worried a lot about me, especially since my parents' death.

"But when I told them I wanted to go, they hugged me close and told me how excited they were that I was going to experience more of the world. They came to visit several times. And that's where I learned how much I loved teaching adults. The students there are so regimented, they work so hard. It was a pleasure being in class every day.

"Of course, I wasn't a full-fledged professor, just an assistant professor. But it was a wonderful time in my life."

"Is that when you got so stubborn?" He grunted when she elbowed him in the stomach. "If it was so great, why did you come home?"

She heaved a heavyhearted sigh. "I missed my family. I was there for over two years, but toward the end, I just knew that God was asking me to come back. I had made some good friends and was dating a great guy…"

Myles felt like she had elbowed him in the gut again. Dating a great guy? Did she still care for him?

"But then Mac got sick."

"Mac is sick?" The man always seemed healthy as a horse and looked better than most men twenty years younger.

"We kept it out of the press. Nana and Mac didn't want it to leak out, afraid it would undermine Mac's position as governor and hurt his next campaign. But he had to have a pacemaker put in when his heart started beating irregularly.

"And after that it was just too hard to be out of the country. I couldn't pass up the opportunity to be close to him, to see him and Nana more often, to let them know how much I love them. There will be more trips abroad, but I only have one set of grandparents."

Her cheek rubbed against his shoulder, and she wiped her eyes with her fingers.

"That must have been rough. I'm sorry."

Sniffling softly, she coughed and continued. "It was a hard time. I hate the thought of not having either Mac or Nana around. I didn't realize how much I relied on them to be around, until there was a possibility that I might lose one of them."

"So then, why the prison?"

"Oh, everyone thought I'd take a job in Salem near Mac and Nana, teaching kindergarten or something like it. But I was hooked on adults after Belgium, so I taught at an adult literacy program for a year. That was the year that the education reform bill passed."

"I can just imagine that Mac was thrilled when you said you wanted to tackle that project." He did not even try to hide the sarcasm in his voice.

"Oh, yes. He practically locked me in the cellar when I mentioned it for the first time." There was a smile in her voice at the memory. "I was surprised when Nana warmed up to the idea long before Mac. But she helped me convince him that I was the best person for the job. He still hates that I work… well, worked there.

"But as soon as I saw how much the inmates needed something to strive for, something to keep them motivated, I was hooked. I know God opened the door for me to teach at the prison, and I'm really glad that He did. There's something really fulfilling about knowing that you're giving some hope to hopeless lives.

"I wasn't free to talk about Jesus in the classroom, but it never stopped me from praying for my students and encouraging them to meet with the chaplain."

"Did you ever pray for me?"

A pretty crimson blush settled onto the only inch of skin on her neck that he could see. "Once or twice, probably."

Not for the first time, he looked at her tiny frame and wondered how she had managed for two years to motivate the hardened felons in the prison. He had lived among them for weeks, and his skin still crawled with the memories of their hatred and bitterness. How had she prayed for these men, cared for them even, when some of them hated her just for being part of the establishment?

"It sounds so cheesy," she sighed, "but God really did give me a love for these men. Most of them just needed to know that someone cared, really cared for them. I hoped that they recognized how much I cared for them by how hard I worked to see them succeed…do you think they did?"

He had only been in her class a couple of days, but Myles was certain she made a difference. "I'm sure that God used you in ways that you won't ever even know."

"Thanks. I needed to hear that today."

They let silence reign for several moments, and soon Kenzie's breathing slowed to an even, steady rhythm, her head tilted back against the gray fabric of the seat and her cheek still brushing his shoulder.

An hour later, as the bus rolled through the outskirts of Salem, his heart still felt twice its normal size. Knowing that she needed him, even if only for words of affirmation, warmed him to the core, gave him strength and a purpose stronger than any assignment ever had. He wanted to hear that she needed him every day. Maybe every day for the rest of his life.

But that meant marriage. Lifetime commitment. The whole deal.

A grin cracked his face.

He'd had much worse ideas than spending his life with Sweet and Spicy Kenzie. With no idea how she had finagled her way so deep into his heart in only eight days, he forced himself to admit that if God placed him on earth to love and serve Kenzie Thorn, that was way more than just okay.

But before he could really consider the life he imagined with her, he had to tell her the truth about Mac.

FIFTEEN

"Kenzie, are you sure you want to do this? Go back into the prison? Go back to your family now?" Myles stabbed his fingers through his hair and pinched his lips together.

"I'm sure. This is the only way to get the proof that we need that JB is behind this entire thing." Her hands were steady, her eyes unwavering.

Myles growled at nothing in particular and glared at a spot on the wall of the bus depot just over her left shoulder. Passengers from the Greyhound that had just exited continued filing by them. "But what if this goes higher than JB? What if…well, what if there are more people involved?" He ignored the fist in his stomach that told him just how bad things were about to get. She would hate him when he explained that this whole thing went so much deeper—or in this case higher—than Kenzie thought. But the stone face of the woman before him reminded him that she would not be easily persuaded to see the reality. If he was going to protect her from Mac, she'd have to know the truth. He had held off talking with her, but it was too late to wait any longer.

She grabbed his hand and held it tightly between both of hers. "Myles, who do you think is involved in this? How could it go any higher than JB? We both agreed that his motive for this must be money. Who else could profit from skimming funds from the education reform budget?"

Myles shrugged. When had he become a coward? A real man would stand up and tell her the truth, tell her that the man she loved more than any other in this world had offered her up as a sacrifice, just to pad his wallet and win an election.

She squeezed his fingers again and looked pleadingly into his eyes. The gray storm there sucked the breath from his lungs and he gasped. She suspected something was amiss—she had to. But the truth could kill her.

"Kenz, I don't—I don't want to be the one to tell you this." He cupped her sun-warmed cheek with his free hand and gazed into her face. This might be his last chance to ever kiss her, so he bent low and pressed his lips firmly to hers. He tried to convey every uncertainty and each certainty through the current that passed between them.

She was pliant in his arms, but he knew that was about to change. He hated this thought so much that he couldn't even enjoy the taste of grape jelly from their breakfast on her lips and the smell of earth and forest clinging to her hair.

Kenzie pulled away and took two deep breaths, her eyes never leaving his. "Tell me what's going on. Tell me now."

"Mac…"

"What about Mac? He's going to understand everything. He'll be on our side."

"I don't think so."

"You don't think he'll understand," she said.

A muscle in Myles's jaw jumped. "I don't think he'll be on our side."

"What?" Kenzie physically jumped back, putting at least two feet of space between them.

Myles grabbed at her hand and clung to it, willing her to understand the words that he was trying to formulate. He tried to pray for the right words, but his thoughts refused to form coherently.

"Kenz, JB is working with Mac. He always has been. Mac is in on the whole thing. I'd bet anything that he knew about JB's plans to have you k—"

"No!"

"Don't you see? I misunderstood Ryker on the phone. I thought he was saying that Mac didn't expect you to be alive because he expected the perpetrators to get rid of you. But he was saying that Mac expected you to die, that he knew the plan was to take you out of the picture."

"Stop it! Stop it! How dare you say such awful things about Mac!" Tears sprang to her eyes and she tugged violently on her hand, trying to remove it from his grasp. Myles looked around at the other bus passengers waiting on benches just outside the small terminal. Many glared reproachfully at him as he clung to her hand. They were going to have to finish this fast, or the police would be called.

"I'm not making this up. This is true. With your death he gets a boost in the governor's race, which we both know he needs. Claudia Suarez isn't making things up or playing games with those TV spots she's campaigning with. Mac needs the pity votes. And with you gone there's no one to immediately look too closely at the money that should be going into the education reform, money that *he* approved, and that he has to know isn't reaching your classroom."

"But there are auditors and people like that who check the budget. They'd notice."

"They should have already noticed. It's been in the budget for two years. Those auditors are hired by the governor's office."

"Well, maybe they just missed it."

Myles groaned and wanted to jab his fingers into his hair and pull it out by the roots. But then he would have to let go of Kenzie's hand, and he couldn't afford to lose their only connection.

"The auditors haven't found it yet because they're being convinced not to find it. If I had to guess, I'd say that Mac is paying them off with some of the money skimmed from the budget, and still making out quite well."

"There! You just said you're guessing! You don't really know what's going on."

"Kenzie! Listen to me!" He raised his voice more than he planned, and took a few breaths to calm down. "Kenz, I'm not guessing here. I'm sure that Mac is part of this. All of it. Everything. Including the plot to have you kidnapped and killed. My supervisor confirmed it."

Kenzie's lip quivered momentarily, and Myles let hope bubble inside him. Hope that she would see his point. Hope that she would be persuaded by the truth. Hope that he hadn't lost her heart.

Seeing his opening, he dove deeper. "Haven't you wondered why we haven't been more ardently pursued? We've barely been noticed by the cops, even when they found the car. We only saw the one article about you in the paper. Why hasn't Mac been tracking us? Don't you think this has been a little too easy?"

But like a child wielding a pin at a balloon, she popped his hope. "You're wrong. How could you even try to pin this on Mac? Maybe you're just jealous of how much he loves me and how much he means to me. Whatever your reason, it doesn't matter." Her eyes were cold as ice, and she yanked her hand hard, dislodging it from his grip.

"Is it so hard for you to imagine that he could fail you, that he might not be as perfect as you always thought?" Myles pleaded.

She flipped her red hair over her shoulder and gave him a

glare that would freeze boiling water. "I hate you for trying to pin this on Mac just because you're jealous of my relationship with him. I will never forgive you for this."

Catching her hand one last time, he pulled her close enough to slip a tiny sheet of paper into her pocket, giving her a way to reach him if she ever changed her mind. He had no real hope. Just ridiculous optimism. A shimmering pool materialized in the corner of her eye just before she turned around and took off down the sidewalk at a dead run.

He sank to the curb, his legs no longer able to hold him. Forgetting every member of their audience, he let tears freely fall into his open hands.

Every moment until Kenzie laid her eyes on their precious faces felt like a whirlwind that would never stop. Running until her side ached so much that she could not go on. Flagging down a passing policeman. The ride to the station. Relentless questions.

"How did you escape?"

"Are you all right?"

"Do you need to go to the hospital?"

"How should we get in contact with your family?"

"Where is the man who did this?"

She could only offer terse answers to the kind-faced policewoman squatting in front of her in the lobby of the station. And oh, how she wanted to answer, to scream the answer to the last question. How dare Myles end it all like this? How could he take everything that they had been through together and throw it away because of his jealousy?

He's at the bus depot! He's just a few miles away! He'll get away! He'll go back to his life as an FBI agent. He'll forget about me and everything we shared.

In that moment of realization, her heart shut down and with

it her mind. She could answer no more questions, could only hug her arms tightly around her middle. But even the soft cotton of the plaid man's shirt she wore reminded her of Myles, of the look of pride on his face when he emerged from the secondhand store with her new wardrobe. Of the way he teasingly tossed her the baseball cap still on her head.

Her stomach ached, and for a moment she thought she would be sick right there on the cold tile floor of the police station, with five officers surrounding her. Head spinning, she excused herself and rushed toward the door marked Women.

Inside the first stall she leaned her forehead against the cool, green metal of the partition, closed her eyes and took several long breaths.

"This isn't happening. This can't be happening," she chanted. "Myles isn't crazy. He didn't just tell me that my grandpa tried to have me killed. He didn't just let me run off alone. It's a dream. This is all just a terrible, terrible dream." As if speaking aloud would somehow make it true, she repeated the last sentence over and over.

It wasn't until she recognized that her shoulders were shaking violently that she realized that tears streamed down her face and sobs interrupted her breathing.

"Oh, God, I can't make any sense out of any of this! Why is this happening to me?" she wailed, anger, frustration and pain erupting from deep in her chest.

"Ms. Thorn, are you okay?" asked the policewoman, who had questioned her in the lobby. The voice sounded near the entrance to the bathroom, and the door groaned as she likely leaned on it.

"Fine. I just need a few moments, please," Kenzie whispered, barely able to hold her emotions in check long enough to respond coherently.

The door creaked closed and Kenzie slid to the floor.

Images from another bathroom scene flashed before her eyes. The disgusting sink. The brown cockroach. Myles holding her to his chest. Their lips pressed together. The pure euphoria of being so protected, cared for so well.

Eyes and throat burning, she hugged her knees to her chest and rocked back and forth on the hard tile. She tried to pray again, but her mind was numb, shut down and overwhelmed with the grief of Myles's betrayal. The minutes sped by before she could finally form a coherent thought. That's when she knew that she really just needed to see Mac, to be held in his arms.

Pushing off from the cold floor and walking out of the stall was easier than she thought it would be. So was washing her face in the sink and walking back into the lobby. With the image of Mac's face in her mind's eye, she moved forward with purpose.

And then she didn't have to imagine him anymore. His strong face, tender with concern, was before her. His sturdy arms wrapped around her. She rested her cheek against his shoulder, only to look into the loving face of Nana. Every gray hair in place, but bottom lip quivering slightly, she put her cool hand on Kenzie's other cheek.

"Honey? Is it really you?"

"I missed you both so much." Kenzie sighed into the cocoon of Mac's arms.

But even though it was the truth, something in the pit of her stomach clenched.

"Nate, I don't know what you want me to say."

"I want you to say that you're keeping an eye on her. I want you to say that you're not giving up on this assignment."

"Fine. I'm not giving up on this assignment. Kenzie Thorn is."

"Borden." The steel in Nate Andersen's voice rose to the

surface. Myles had learned long before not to cross his direct supervisor, the special agent in charge of the Portland office. Nate was a man of impeccable morals, tough as nails and smarter than any other man Myles had met in the Bureau. That was why he had been promoted so quickly through the ranks, being in charge of the Portland office when he was just over thirty years old. "Tell me what happened with Thorn. Why didn't you bring her to the safe house in the first place?"

"I told you when I called in days ago. It got complicated."

"Complicated," Andersen said. He meant *unacceptable.*

Myles shot his hand through his hair and grumbled under his breath. "There was the mountain lion attack. And then she was so set on going with me that I was afraid that she'd blow the whole thing if I left her alone. As long as she was with me, I figured I had it under control."

Andersen cleared his throat. "Is she with you now?"

"No." Although Nate could not see him through the phone line, Myles hung his head in appropriate shame. He continued staring at his feet as he walked back and forth on the plush carpet of the hotel room. His current living situation was a far cry from the cabin, the Evergreen Motel and the Jewel. In fact, it was nicer than his apartment in Portland. But it was a temporary fix. A place for him to clear his mind and figure out his next move.

Which was why he'd called his supervisor in the first place. But the guilt over losing Kenzie's confidence and her heart killed his will to continue. He would rather sit on the floor at the foot of the king-size bed and think about wild auburn hair and stormy-gray eyes than think about the futility of trying to get back into her good graces.

"Myles! Snap out of it!" Nate's voice ripped him from his wandering thoughts. "It's my job to see you succeed on this assignment. I believe that you can do that. And I'm going to help you."

"What are you thinking?"

"We need to get proof. We need a wire tap on Mac's personal and business phones. But we need some evidence against him before we can even get that."

Myles frowned. "What about the budget numbers? If we can get the budget sheet from Kenzie's desk at the prison, then I think I know what judge will give us a warrant to tap Mac's phones."

Myles could almost hear Nate's smile, which matched his own. "Claudia Suarez," they said at the same time.

"Can you lend me a hand with getting the budget from Kenzie's desk?" Myles asked.

"As a matter of fact, I can. The prison was looking to re-place Kenzie fast. They were interviewing teachers two days after her kidnapping. As usual, I was on top of it and got a new agent set up in the position. She already has the budget in hand, given to her by Ryker on the first day of work. I'm going to fax over the warrant to request paperwork right now along with the budget. Get it filled out and ready to submit first thing in the morning."

"Will do."

"Oh, and Myles?"

"Yes, sir?"

"Figure out what you're going to do about your feelings for Kenzie. Then do it."

"Feelings?" He should have known he could not hide his affection for Kenzie, especially from Nate.

"I'm not stupid. Just make up your mind and do it. The same way you went after law school and Quantico."

"I will."

"Good man."

"But I doubt Kenzie will be at the governor's mansion. They'll want to keep her out of the spotlight for a while."

"Then it's a good thing you work for the FBI," Andersen

said, not hiding his sarcasm. "I'll make a call in the morning and get back to you."

"Thank you."

"Get some sleep, Borden. You're going to need it to nail the governor."

Myles hung up the phone and began pacing again. He loved being right, and he was about to get the proof that he needed that Mac was crooked, that he was the man behind the entire plot to kidnap and kill Kenzie. He knew that proving he was right would not return him to Kenzie's good graces. Likely it would only drive the wedge between them even deeper. But even if the truth hurt her, destroyed their relationship, at least it would keep her safe. She would be safe. Curled up on a fluffy couch, her hair spilled over the white fabric. Tucked beneath a green-and-gray quilt. Sleeping soundly. Safely.

As Myles sank to the floor and rested his face in his palms, his thoughts consumed him. He cared more that the truth would keep Kenzie safe than that it meant successfully completing his assignment. He cared more about Kenzie's feelings of loss than he did about his own personal victory.

This had all started out as a job. A simple undercover assignment. The same as any other. Get in. Get the job done right. Get out. For years that routine had given him a purpose. He felt that God had called him to serve in this way. But he'd never let another assignment reach him so deeply. He'd kept them all at arm's length, believing that he needed the emotional distance to do his duty.

So why did he now feel like he could never do his job again—without his most recent assignment close by his side?

He couldn't pinpoint exactly when it happened, but with her wild, red hair and spitfire attitude to match, Kenzie had snuck into his heart. She consumed his waking thoughts, and without her, his life felt a little emptier. The way it had felt right after his mom's parents had died—only worse than then. And he'd only known Kenzie for a couple weeks.

Oh, he was definitely in over his head.

God, he prayed silently, his head resting in the palms of his hands, *I'm in love with this woman. I can't imagine my life without her. But even if our relationship never recovers, even if it's not Your plan for us to be together, please protect her. Protect her heart from the ache that is coming, from the pain that is about to land in her lap.*

But if it might be possible, please help her to see that I'm doing what I have to do to see that the truth comes to light. Please help her to see how much I care for her, how much I want to be with her, how much I want to protect her and keep her safe. Just let her love me the way that I love her.

And there they were, all of his feelings freely admitted to God and to himself. He left them in God's hands. Left God to figure out how He would work everything out. It wasn't his to worry about anymore. He knew these things in his heart, deep in his gut. But even as he filled out the paperwork that came through the fax machine, his mind worried about what would happen, what would come of his feelings for Kenzie Thorn.

Late that night, when he finally crawled into the big, soft bed, he dreamed dreams of red hair and gray eyes and soft pink lips. And even in his dreams he feared that he had lost his chance to be with the woman he loved.

SIXTEEN

Kenzie snuggled deeper into the enormous sectional that took up almost the entire family room in her childhood home. Tucked beneath one of Nana's handmade quilts and sipping Nana's famous hot cocoa, she felt almost normal. Henry, Nana's little bichon, jumped into her lap and reached up to lick her cheek with his rough tongue. She slid her hands along the silk of his fur and nuzzled his neck.

"I've missed you, buddy," she whispered for his ears alone. He cocked his head to one side and let out a quiet ruff. Oh, how she had missed everything that Henry represented. When Mac won his first term as governor, Nana refused to even take Henry to visit the governor's mansion.

"Henry and I will stay here, thank you," she had said in a tone that brooked no argument, even from the new governor. "We are not giving up the only home that Kenzie can remember. So we'll keep both houses." And they had. They kept this house, the one Kenzie moved into after her parents' deaths, and Henry stayed with Nana. They threw the required events and parties at Mahonia Hall, the official governor's residence, but Henry always stayed at this home on the outskirts of the city. Where Henry lived was Nana's home. And Mac stayed as close to Nana as he could, too, especially since he was diagnosed with his heart condition.

Now Henry circled her lap twice, then settled down, resting his little head against her knee. The pink tip of his tongue licked his lips as he let out a soft sigh.

She scratched him behind his ears and he perked up for a moment, looking around the room, but finally settling in completely. His warm little body felt normal. It was all so normal. Almost like the last eight days had been a dream.

The bedroom she grew up in was still the same, with pink walls and a fuchsia bedspread. The closet still held some of her clothes left over from her irregular trips from Evergreen. In it she found a comfy pair of women's jeans and a roomy college sweatshirt. It was blissful to wear clothes that fit like they should, hugging her hips and thighs, not billowing around her like the men's jeans she wore for almost a week.

Now, after a restful night of sleep in a familiar bed, sitting cross-legged on the couch, wrapped in handmade comfort, snuggling with her favorite four-legged friend and feeling like herself for the first time in over a week, she felt a little lost. She felt oddly disconnected from the old Kenzie. The Kenzie that had never been kidnapped. The Kenzie that had never met Myles Borden. The Kenzie that could be comforted by a simple hug from Mac.

The trouble was that her stomach tightened every time she thought about the words that Myles had said about Mac. Of course they could not be completely true. But what if there was a shred of truth to them? What if he was partly right? What if Mac wasn't as blameless as she wanted him to be?

In the middle of begging God for wisdom about the entire situation, Kenzie was startled when Nana entered the family room and sat right next to her. Her eyes looked heavy, pained, and the wrinkles at the corners of her mouth looked more pronounced than usual. Nana pulled Kenzie's hand from Henry's soft curls and into both of her hands. Her cool fingers gently stroked the back of Kenzie's.

"I wanted to talk to you while Mac is at the store this morning," Nana began.

"What's going on?"

Nana looked at their intertwined hands as though deep in thought. She attempted to look into Kenzie's eyes, but only made it to the tip of her nose before shifting her gaze back to their hands. "Did—that man—the one who kidnapped you—"

Kenzie had been quite certain that they would want to know everything about her time with Myles. She just had no idea how to explain it. Honesty always being the best policy seemed the likely route. With a few minor omissions. Like that kiss that she and Myles shared in the disgusting hotel bathroom. And the one the day before her birthday. And that look that always appeared in his eyes when he cupped her cheek with his calloused hand. And the way he made her heart beat three times faster than normal just by squeezing her hand.

She would leave those things out to spare Nana's poor heart. And her own embarrassment.

Of course, Mac and Nana both knew what she had told the police officers the day before. Clinging to Mac's hand, she had calmly explained how she had clubbed her abductor, Myles Parsons, over the head with a fire extinguisher and been able to escape from the Salem hotel room where he held her hostage. She had never seen any indication of which hotel she had been staying in. But likely Myles would already be on his way to Canada.

At least that's how she explained the ordeal to the kind policewoman squatting by her side.

Nana cleared her throat softly, now looking at the plush

carpet, one of her hands cupping Henry's head. "What I mean to say—did that man hurt you, in any way? You can be completely honest with me."

Kenzie squeezed her hand into her grandmother's. "No. He didn't hurt me at all."

Unless you count breaking my heart.

"You can tell me. *Anything.*"

How tempting to let it all pour from her mouth. The things she was certain of, like JB's part in her abduction, Myles's integrity and how she cared more for Myles than any man she had ever met.

Instead she bit her tongue. JB Ryker was a family friend. And Nana was not prepared to hear about how Kenzie had fallen for her kidnapper.

"Nana, I'm fine. Myles Parsons never hurt me. In fact, he saved me from a mountain lion."

"A mountain lion in Salem?"

Kenzie coughed. "It was before we got to Salem. Near Evergreen. He risked his life to save me."

"But why would he kidnap you, take you from us and save your life, but never ask for ransom? It doesn't make any sense." Now she looked into Kenzie's eyes, the confusion evident on her face.

"He rarely did."

"What do you mean?"

Kenzie was the one to drop her gaze this time. "I just mean that he was a bit of an enigma. He took good care of me, but he insisted that I could not return to you or the prison."

"Well, then, he and your grandfather have at least one thing in common. Mac has downright refused to let you go back to that place."

Kenzie's heart rate picked up, and her stomach knotted. The proof that they—she, she had to remember that she was alone now—needed about the budget was in her desk at work. She had to get back there.

"But I have—I left some things in my desk. I need to get them."

"Oh, the prison already sent over your lesson plan book and everything else from your desk. JB sent it as soon as the new teacher was hired. Didn't you see the box in your room?"

"A new teacher was hired? So soon?"

"You know that the other state prisons are counting on Evergreen's second year of successful program completion. They had to keep getting those boys through the exam preparations or it would have toppled the entire program."

"Yes, but a replacement? Why didn't they just hire a substitute? Or have someone from the Department of Corrections fill in?"

"You know how the red tape is with security. I guess they decided it would be easier to just hire someone new. On top of that, no one expected that you'd want to return. You don't, do you?"

Kenzie stood quickly—sending Henry jumping to the ground with a yip and circling her ankles—and set her mug of cocoa on a coaster on the end table. "Of course I do." Taking a steadying breath, she said, "Excuse me, please." Forcing her feet to make smooth, even strides toward her bedroom, she attempted her exit.

Just before she rounded the corner into the hallway, Nana called out, "Sweetie, we're expecting someone from the phone company today. If the doorbell rings and I'm in the back garden, please let him in and show him the phone in the kitchen and the one in your grandfather's study."

"Yes, ma'am."

Within seconds Kenzie knelt beside a box of files sitting at the foot of her bed. She blamed her ignorance of the presence of this box the night before on exhaustion. Tearing through each file, she hunted for the prison budget she had been given. Tucked safely into a folder next to her student files, just where she had placed it almost a year before, was the budget information, stamped CONFIDENTIAL.

The measly annual budget numbers glared back up at her. She knew who needed this information. And she knew how to contact him.

Inside the pocket of the jeans she had thrown on the floor the night before lay a scrap of paper with a phone number on it. She dug into the pocket until her fingers grasped the little slip. In blocky handwriting, Myles had written her a note.

For anything you need 24/7—555-9347.

Could she do it? Could she call him after storming away from him the way she had? He needed this information. Even if he was wrong about Mac, the truth about JB Ryker needed to be known, and this was his proof.

Four digits into dialing the phone number, the doorbell rang. Then immediately again, like the person could not wait for a moment. Henry barked, and she heard him scamper toward the front door.

Deciding Myles could wait for a few seconds, she hopped up and ran to the front door. Two men in service uniforms held ID badges out at her.

"I'm John. This is Teddy," said the shorter of the two. The larger man did indeed seem to be a teddy-bear sort, round, congenial and silent. "We're from the phone company. We've had several complaints about service in this neighborhood, so we need to check on both of your lines."

Kenzie nodded, opening the door wide enough for them to step into the foyer. As she moved to close it, her eyes played a trick on her. She thought she saw Myles sitting in a truck at the end of the driveway. But of course that was an illusion.

He couldn't really be there; and anyway, she could not possibly recognize Myles from a hundred feet away.

But there was no telling her heart that. It pounded wildly at the mere thought of him being so close. Perhaps she should let her heart settle down before actually calling him.

Myles had nodded at John and Teddy as they walked past his rented pickup truck a minute before. From the white FBI van with a local phone company's logo splashed across the sides, they had entered the governor's house, the house that right now sheltered Kenzie Thorn.

Lucky bums.

Of course, they were the best men for the job. The most technologically advanced agents in the state, and not half-bad actors. They were still in the governor's second residence, which was likely his primary home, placing three miniscule bugs to pick up both sides of every phone conversation in the house, as well as any audio from the governor's personal office. And in about fifteen minutes John and Teddy would return to the van, take it for a spin around the block and arrive at the same spot with a new facade-free vehicle to record every minute of every conversation in the house.

Thank you, Claudia Suarez. She had just earned his vote. And thank you, John and Teddy.

His mind wandered to what Kenzie looked like today. Dressed in feminine clothes and really clean for the first time in days, her red hair curly and smelling of that perfume she wore the first day he met her. Not that she didn't always smell good, even when they roughed it in the cabin or picked their way through clues in Evergreen. But that lemon-lime scent that she wore at the prison was bliss.

A groan from deep in his throat echoed in the cab of the truck, and he leaned his head back against the seat. *It's me again, God. Still begging for You to work something out for me and Kenzie. Any help here would be great, so that we can have a chance to see if this is really what You want. But no matter what, thanks for getting us safely this far.* These short bursts of prayer were becoming more and more frequent the longer he went without seeing her stormy-gray eyes, sweet-and-spicy smile and wild curls.

The minutes passed achingly slowly as he sat in his truck. He could not afford to be distracted by the radio, so it remained in the off position. Both windows were opened a crack so that he could feel a slight breeze, but as the sun rose nearer its zenith, the stagnant heat became almost unbearable. Sweat dripped down his temples and the back of his neck, yet he sat still, only staring at the gray house across the street, wondering how much longer John and Teddy would be inside.

The cell phone in his pocket rang three times before the sound penetrated his consciousness, he was so focused on Kenzie's home. On the fourth chime, he flicked it open. "Borden."

"Um…Myles?"

His heart exploded. "Kenzie! I'm so glad you called! How are you?" He sat a little taller, and if possible, stared a little harder at the front door of the house.

"I'm—I'm fine, I guess." She sounded uncertain, scared, anything but the strong woman he had grown to care for.

"Kenzie, what's going on? I didn't think you'd call."

She paused. "I wasn't going to. It's just that I have the proof that we talked about. I have the budget from the prison. And even though you're wrong about Mac, it can help you take down JB."

He longed to see her face, to watch her forehead wrinkle and her nostrils flare when she spoke Ryker's name. But how could he respond to her offer? He already had the budget, and he was more convinced than ever that Mac was behind the conspiracy to have her killed. But he hadn't seen her face in more than twenty-four long hours.

"Thank you. It means a lot to me that you're still willing to help me. Can we arrange a drop-off?"

"I can't very well let Ryker off the hook, can I? He had me kidnapped." The tenor of her voice rose in strength, and he could almost hear the beginning of a smile.

"It wasn't that bad, was it?"

Now she laughed. "Aside from the indescribable fear when I realized I wasn't alone in my car, the mountain lion attack, being chased by cops and having to nurse you back to health at every bend in the road, it wasn't the worst thing ever."

"You make me out to be some kind of sickly wimp. I was injured. Saving your life, I might add."

She grew soft-spoken again. "I know. And I never minded. After I decided you didn't deserve to have me run over you with the car, anyway."

"You were going to run me over?" he asked.

"The thought crossed my mind."

"I'm glad you didn't go through with it."

"Me, too."

Silence hung over the phone line. With no clue what to say, Myles cleared his throat. Kenzie did not take the hint that she should pick up the conversation by offering her undying devotion and showering him with words of her affection.

"So how should we do this drop-off?" she finally asked.

"There's a little coffee shop at the corner of Main Street and Fourth Avenue called Buster's."

"Yes, I know it. I have to wait until some phone company repair guys are done. But I can be there by one o'clock."

"Okay. I'll see you there."

"Oh, Myles…"

"Yeah?"

"Be careful, okay? There are still pictures of you in the paper here. I told them you were probably in Canada by now. But just in case, be careful."

She ended the call, and he sat with a silly grin spread across his face that he could not get rid of. So she hadn't told the police where to find him when they parted ways.

She had told him in that roach-infested bathroom that he'd earned a kiss from her. Well, she had certainly just earned one from him, and he never reneged on a debt.

Leaning back, he rested his hands behind his head and smiled at the gray house across the street. He would wait until she left, then follow her to the coffee shop. Until then, he would just enjoy the sunshine and the thought of paying her what she was due.

"Kenzie, I'm going to the store. Do you need anything?" Nana's head poked through the crack between Kenzie's bedroom door and the frame. "Mac just returned home. He's in his office."

Kenzie could not help but smile at the older woman's face. Though the years—and especially the last week of stress—increased the lines and wrinkles on her face, her smile was always contagious, reaching to her eyes and enhancing the crow's-feet there.

Kenzie returned Nana's smile and reached down to scratch Henry behind his ears. "Good boy." He perked up even more at the sound of her voice and nuzzled her calf through the jeans she wore.

To her grandmother she replied, "I'm fine. Did the phone company guys leave yet?"

Nana mumbled something under her breath in a huff. "They just left a minute ago."

"Okay. I'll see you later." Kenzie sat down on her bed and

patted her thighs to get Henry's attention. He leaped to her lap and put his front paws onto her shoulders as she scratched his sides. His little white doggy face looked into hers with pure contentment in his eyes. The front door opened and closed, and Kenzie heard Nana's car pulling down the long driveway. "Do you think I should have told her that I'm going to meet up with a friend this afternoon?"

Henry barked. Kenzie's stomach danced with butterflies.

"Me neither. She wouldn't understand. At least not yet. But this does put us in a bit of a predicament as far as transportation goes." Holding Henry close to her chest, she walked down the hallway and into the foyer, the socks on her feet muffling each step on the hardwood floor.

One peek out the window next to the door confirmed what Kenzie already knew. The only vehicle in the driveway was Mac's shining silver Cadillac Escalade. She had teased him, when he bought it three months before, that it made him look like some kind of drug cartel baron. He had chuckled and said only that he and Nana had been saving for a new car, and they had enough to splurge.

Her forehead wrinkled as she thought about the SUV. Complete with all the bells and whistles, it was quite a sight. Mac and Nana would have had to pay well over $40,000 to buy it outright. Mac and Nana lived modestly. Nana had never worked, for as long as Kenzie could remember. And Mac earned very little as the governor, in comparison to the responsibilities required of him.

Kenzie's stomach clenched as she saw Myles's face in her mind's eye. The pure truth radiating from his voice as he told her the very last thing in the world she wanted to believe.

"Could Myles possibly be right?" she asked Henry. He looked at her quizzically, then put his cold, wet nose into her neck.

She had to talk to Myles, and a glance at her watch told her that she needed to leave shortly to meet him at the coffeehouse as they planned. But she needed to borrow Mac's Escalade to get anywhere. Her own car was likely still at the cabin. But borrowing the car meant speaking directly to Mac. Alone.

Henry barked suddenly and jumped to the floor, running for the back door. He pushed at it with his nose until she let him out. She stepped outside and watched him run behind a bush and just a few seconds later return, as excited as ever to see her. He jumped at her knees until she scooped him back up.

"Shall we go see about borrowing Mac's car?" she asked Henry. She moved toward the front of the house, strangely nervous to be alone with Mac for the first time. Heart thudding with each step, she made her way toward the dark maple door of Mac's study. She reached for the doorknob with a shaking hand, the other holding tightly to Henry.

"You're being silly," she whispered to herself, clenching her free hand and taking a deep breath. A calmer hand clamped around the doorknob and turned it silently. The heavy door slid open a fraction of an inch, revealing the sunlit study filled with a maple desk and bookcase set.

Reclining in the huge leather chair behind the desk, Mac sat with his back to the door, and he did not turn. It took several seconds for her to realize that he wasn't alone in the room, but she couldn't see who he was speaking to through the narrow crack in the door.

His hand shot through his silver hair in a motion not unlike a familiar one of Myles's. "Okay, okay! You said you would work this out. But I never wanted Kenzie to get hurt. You said we'd just pay off that guard to keep his mouth shut, and then you were going to hunt down this inmate and take care of him. Kenzie was supposed to return to us unharmed within a day, but too scared to ever return to the prison. But that's not what's happened at all! Where did your plan go awry?"

"My plan didn't go awry. It just changed." The voice was gravelly, and Kenzie would have recognized it anywhere.

"What do you mean by that, Joe?" Mac jumped to his feet and crossed the room in the direction of JB's voice.

"Just what I said. She had to be taken out of the picture. You and I both know there's not enough money to fund your campaign against someone with deep pockets like Suarez's husband without our extra prison income. And you know that the minute that Claudia Suarez is elected, she'll start looking into the prison reform…so that could land you without a job and likely behind bars. And your granddaughter was getting mighty interested in the budget. One request to the legislature, and she would have blown the whole thing wide-open."

"Right. Which was why we were going to scare Kenzie away. Not kill her!" Mac's voice grew angry and loud.

"Are you willing to risk the election because Kenzie suddenly got nosy? I didn't think so. And we both know you'd never risk turning me in." His laugh was nasty and vicious, and Kenzie could almost see the brutality reflected in his eyes. "You and me, Macky, we're the same kind. Hungry for money and the power that money buys."

Mac sighed, as though resigning himself to the truth of JB's words. "Well, she's back now. And safe. But what about the inmate? Have you heard anything from him? Or Larry?"

JB cleared his throat. "Not yet. But we'll find them, and take care of both of them—permanently. We can't have it leaking out that they were hired to kidnap Kenzie and take care of her."

Mac mumbled something too quietly for her to hear. Or maybe her heartbeats were so loud they blocked out any other sound. *It was true. All of it!* What Myles had said about Mac being involved in the entire plot. And they were still after him. They were going to kill him!

In a single instant the world flew apart. Henry jumped from Kenzie's arms, darting into the study. A car horn outside honked wildly. And Mac spun around, his eyes, so similar to hers, locking onto her gaze.

JB jumped from somewhere behind Mac's much larger frame and seemed to cross the room in one motion. Her left arm ached, and it was a full second before she realized that it was because his wiry hand was clamped around it.

"How much did you hear?" JB's voice, suddenly unfamiliar, sounded smooth as silk.

In spite of violently shaking knees, she sent up a silent, confused prayer. In the past, she always prayed that God would send Mac to rescue her. But how could she pray for that now, when the men she needed rescuing from were JB and Mac himself?

God, Myles was right, and I was so wrong. I have no one to rely on but You! Please don't fail me now!

JB shook her arm and growled again, "How much?"

Several yards behind JB, Mac's eyes held her gaze, but the light that had once shone in them had disappeared. His always-strong shoulders slumped slightly, defeated.

With quivering lips she replied, "Enough."

"Well, that won't do." JB's lips twisted cruelly as his grip tightened. A mean-looking pistol materialized in his hand, likely from his waistband, where his suit coat had covered it. He twisted her arm behind her back and shoved the gun into the soft tissue of her back until she winced and Mac took a step forward.

"What are you doing, Joe?"

"Well, she obviously has to be disposed of. She knows too much!"

Mac jumped at the harsh words. "That's crazy. She's my granddaughter! She won't say anything. Just put the gun away."

Kenzie took a deep breath, trying to calm her wild nerves, but it only served to press the cold muzzle of the gun farther into her back. "Superintendent Ryker, please, I won't say anything. I promise."

"No one needs to get hurt here. This is just about money. It was never supposed to get this deep. It just got out of hand. It's just money. It's not worth it," Mac said, taking baby steps toward her and JB.

"Not worth it?" JB exploded, his breath thick and hot on the back of her neck. "This girl is threatening my position and my reputation, and you say dispatching her isn't worth it! Hah! She has to be taken care of, and you know it! Her testimony sends you and I both to prison for a long time. Do you know what it's like for a prison superintendent on the inside?"

Kenzie could just imagine the torture of that situation. But for the moment it paled in comparison to her own terror. This was the end of her life. She was pretty sure she wouldn't live to see Myles or Nana again. And it broke her heart.

God, save me! He's going to kill me! Kenzie's heart cried as JB brought the gun around to her side and something in the house suddenly exploded.

SEVENTEEN

Myles's fingers drummed ceaselessly on the steering wheel of the truck. No particular rhythm, he just needed some sound to fill the emptiness.

Suddenly he spied Teddy and his partner exiting the house and crossing the street. The big man nodded at Myles, signaling that the bugs had been planted.

A glance at the dashboard and the clock read 12:43 p.m. Kenzie should be leaving now. Any minute. The phone repair guys had just left. She should be free to head toward their meeting.

The front door opened, and his heart leapt. But it was Kenzie's grandmother going to her sedan and pulling it onto the street—leaving Kenzie and Mac alone in the house.

Kenzie was alone with Mac.

Mac would not be crazy enough to hurt Kenzie in his own home. Would he?

12:44 p.m. Still no sign of Kenzie.

His thumbs joined the percussion section on his steering wheel to the rhythm of his high school's fight song. Strange that it should pop into his mind now, but he felt the same way he always had before a big game. Breathing slow. Heart beating steadily quicker and quicker.

He scratched his right thigh. The doctor at the twenty-four-hour urgent care had told him that the mountain lion wound was mending at a good rate, and the fact that it itched constantly was a sign that it was healing. The chances of it reopening were very low, and there was no infection. Although he would likely always have a scar, it would diminish with time. All in all, the doctor praised the care that it had received.

Myles conveniently failed to mention that he had managed to rip it open several times since the original attack. Instead, he focused on remembering the way that Kenzie had cared for him, even when she thought him a felon who intended to kill her. She was something else, so tender and spunky. His Sweet and Spicy Kenzie.

12:46 p.m.

Still no sign of her.

If she didn't leave right away, she'd never make it to the coffeehouse in time to meet him at one, like they arranged. What could be holding her up?

He opened the door of the truck to check in with the van fifty yards down the street, but quickly slammed it shut when another car pulled into the driveway. Not Mrs. Thorn's car. This one a sleek, black Lincoln Town Car. When it stopped, a driver got out and stepped to the back door, opening it. Out stepped JB Ryker. The man who had tried to have Kenzie taken out of the picture. JB looked around the street quickly, then walked to the front door, letting himself in without knocking.

The silence in the cab of his truck was deafening. He would have given anything to hear what the bug was picking up in Mac's office. But where was Kenzie in the house? Was she okay, or being detained against her will?

The unknown was killing Myles, so after another minute he hopped out of the cab of the truck and strolled toward

Teddy and John's van, trying not to attract attention from the neighbors. At least he'd be able to hear some of what was happening in the house from there. But before he made it halfway to them, the van's horn honked in three rapid beeps. Teddy and John leaped from the van and darted toward him. He instantly spun and raced for the front door of the house.

There could be only one reason for their actions. They had the information they needed to prosecute Mac and JB Ryker. And someone was in trouble inside that house.

The only person at risk was Kenzie.

Running on complete instinct, Myles hurdled the hedge and reached the front door moments before his fellow special agents. No time to pick the lock, he lifted his left leg and kicked right below the door handle. His foot smarted, and his old knee injury screamed. The door barely budged.

One more attempt and then he was going to have to pull his gun. Lucky for the door, it splintered away from the frame the second time his boot struck it.

Someone yelped down the hallway, and he raced in that direction, John and Teddy right behind him. Myles pulled his weapon from his shoulder holster and held it in front of him with locked elbows.

At every turn he feared seeing Kenzie lying on the floor, injured or worse. His mind shut down from fear, and he acted only on training, sweeping into every room and checking for occupants.

It seemed an eternity before Myles plowed into a room that looked like a study with an enormous desk and bookshelves full of leather-bound volumes. JB, Kenzie and her grandfather stood in the middle of the room. JB's outraged expression and dangerously waving weapon described the situation perfectly.

"Do you know who I am?" JB demanded.

Kenzie winced as the pistol in JB's hand grazed her chin,

and Myles noticed for the first time that Mac seemed stunned by the entire situation.

Hands steady around the butt of his weapon, Myles took a deep breath. "Let her go."

"Get out of here! This has nothing to do with you!" JB's anger filled every corner of the room like a deluge. He was too distracted to take a close look at the man holding the weapon, and Myles was thankful that JB didn't seem to recognize him from their two brief encounters inside the prison.

Kenzie's eyes, wide with fear, jumped from Myles to Teddy to John. "Please—please help me," she begged, at the same time taking a step away from JB.

Teddy took the opportunity to pull out his badge and make introductions. "I'm Special Agent Theodore Dawson. These are Special Agents Myles Borden and John Timmins. Sir, please put the gun down and step away from the lady."

For a split second Myles thought that JB would refuse, would put up a fight, but he never had a chance. With the same agility she had shown when she kicked Myles in the cabin, Kenzie lifted her foot and kicked it backward into Ryker's kneecap. The older man screamed in pain and dropped his hold on her arm. Teddy easily swiped the gun from Ryker's hand as he rolled on the floor, holding his leg.

The rage on Ryker's face slowly dissipated as the truth of the situation hit him. His eyes squinted as he looked up at Kenzie and the three FBI special agents.

Kenzie had lunged forward, crawling to the wall, and she pulled her knees to her chin. A small white dog nuzzled her side.

Teddy took a breath and said something that Myles guessed he had never thought he would have to say in his lifetime. "Governor Thorn, Superintendent Ryker, you're both under arrest for embezzling government funds and for conspiracy to commit murder."

Mac's head shook side to side, and he tried to explain. "I never meant for it to go this far. Kenzie, you have to believe me." He looked into Kenzie's face, but her expression was rigid, frozen in fear, eyes eclipsing the rest of her features.

Lowering his weapon, Myles pulled her to her feet and away from the scene where Teddy handcuffed Mac and Ryker while John read them their Miranda Rights.

Myles fought every internal instinct to pull her into his arms and comfort her. He had already ruined his professional reputation with her, taking advantage of her while they were on their own in Evergreen. But now he kept at least a foot between them as she stared unblinkingly at the scene in the middle of the room. He doubted his touch would be of any comfort after the way they parted at the bus station. His embrace now would only serve to rub in the truth of her grandfather's betrayal.

When Muriel Thorn arrived back at the house, her husband was just being led to the police car that had been called as backup. Knowing enough to give the women their privacy, Myles exited the house as Kenzie fell into her grandmother's waiting arms.

Kenzie clung to Nana's arm in shock as they walked down the driveway past the elaborate SUV that now Kenzie realized surely had been purchased with money from the prison budget. They followed Mac as one of the FBI agents led him toward the black-and-white police car blocking the end of the driveway. Another police car, holding JB, and several other sedans, likely unmarked police vehicles, filled the street.

Kenzie sighed in relief that none of the neighbors poked their heads out of front doors or peeked obviously between blinds. Watching Mac with his head hung low and wrists cuffed behind his back was hard enough without an audience.

This kind of humiliation would ruin Nana's reputation and could leave her without a single friend. How could Mac possibly do that to her? To both of them?

A uniformed police officer opened the back door of the black-and-white, while the special agent leading him placed his hand on top of Mac's head. Mac took the moment to glance over his shoulder, looking from Nana to Kenzie, meeting each of their gazes.

"I'm sorry," he said. He neither shouted nor whispered, but his voice easily carried the twenty feet between them. "I've made some terrible mistakes."

"I have, too," Nana whispered.

The special agent said, "Sir, you still have the right to remain silent. Anything you say can and will be used against you in a court of a law."

Never taking his gaze off of Nana, Mac replied, "I'm aware of that, but some things need to be said. Muriel, please forgive me. I've been so blind. I never—I never meant for Kenzie to get involved in this. You both are the most important things in my life. But I'm nothing if I'm not the governor. I'm not worthy of you without this position. I needed the money for the campaign. Suarez was doing too well. I needed the money! Can't you understand that? I never thought that Joe would take it so far, putting Kenzie in danger. I was just trying to protect her, getting her out of the prison."

Nana shuddered, and Kenzie pulled her a little closer to her side, wrapping an arm around her shoulders. As the agent helped Mac into the backseat, Nana whispered, "I never cared about the governorship." She spoke so softly that Mac had no chance of hearing it, but Kenzie heard it clearly.

Pulling her grandmother into a tight embrace, Kenzie let two teardrops slip down her cheeks. "Nana, I'm sorry."

Nana held on to the back of Kenzie's shirt with all the

strength in her frail hands, clutching the fabric into fist-shaped wrinkles. "No, I'm sorry, dear."

"This isn't your fault."

"I should have done more."

"What do you mean?"

Nana's shoulders shook as she cried silently. "I knew, just knew that there was something wrong. I was worried about you working at the prison, and then I overheard Mac on the phone several months ago. I couldn't sit back and do nothing, so I called my friend Nate Andersen."

The name sounded familiar to Kenzie, but she couldn't place where she had heard it before. As though reading her thoughts, Nana continued, "Nate is the special agent in charge of the Portland office of the FBI. He and I met at a law enforcement fund-raiser several years ago. He was very kind to me, so when I thought you were in serious danger, I called him to make sure that you'd be protected."

"You asked the FBI to watch out for me? You're the reason that Myles kidnapped me?"

Nana shrugged slightly, her eyes sad. "I'm sorry, honey. I should have done more. I just didn't know who else to go to."

Kenzie could hardly believe her ears. "But why didn't you tell me?"

"Well, I didn't know how extreme Nate would be, putting one of his men undercover. And of course I had no idea that you'd be kidnapped. What possible reason could it serve to worry you? What if it all had nothing to do with you? You would have been frightened for no reason." Kenzie blanched at her reasoning, almost laughing out loud. Nana patted her hand. "Now, now. Everything has worked out, hasn't it? God's brought us through this mess in one piece."

Kenzie looked down the driveway as the police cars carrying Mac and JB pulled into the street. It all seemed unreal—

like a dream, only with real consequences that would likely see her grandfather locked in prison.

Tears filled her eyes and she reached for her grandmother. "Thank you for what you did."

Nana nodded into Kenzie's shoulder, and the two women held onto each other as though they might never let go. Kenzie could only hold on tight and wait for the emotions to calm. She needed to be strong, but the truth was that she craved the feel of strong, protective arms cradling her to an immovable chest. Arms that comforted in the face of the truth.

She had been betrayed for money and the governor's race.

Looking over Nana's shoulder, Kenzie searched the faces of the FBI agents and police officers milling around the driveway. Myles was nowhere to be found. No shaggy brown hair or piercing blue eyes.

Likely never again.

Kenzie slid into the pew beside her grandmother, the same pew they had shared at First Grace for nearly twenty years. It was more than a week after Mac's arrest, and the memories of that horrific day still made her ache to her very core. She bowed her head, with no words to pray, and just sat silently, hoping for a peace that passed all understanding. At length, her grandmother squeezed her hand gently, and Kenzie looked into the kind old face.

"Sweetie, you must stop beating yourself up over this. Your grandfather made his own decisions. As much as we'd like to, we can't control the actions of the ones we love."

Kenzie swallowed deeply, guilt flooding through her. But not guilt for Mac's actions. Guilt that she was only concerned with her own broken heart.

Myles had stood right next to her that day in Mac's study and barely touched her. He never held her. Never comforted her. Apparently never cared for her. And she was left with a broken heart, for she had been forced to admit that Myles had never lied. Not about Mac or his motives. The money, the power, the election, he'd risked her for all of it.

The truth about Mac stung. But the truth about Myles broke her.

God, mend my broken heart. If I never see Myles again, let me know that I'm okay with You alone. But if You wouldn't mind, I'd really like to see him again. Please.

And then, as if he appeared because she prayed for him to, Myles strode down the far aisle of the sanctuary. He slipped into the row behind them, sitting in the farthest seat away from her.

When he looked up and met her eyes with his blue gaze, her breath vanished and she whipped her head around to stare at the large cross hanging in the front of the vast room.

When Pastor Peter began his sermon, Kenzie could barely hear the words he spoke for the rushing in her ears. The sound of butterfly wings. The butterflies that swarmed her stomach as she felt Myles's gaze lock onto her neck.

Legs bouncing and heart racing, she barely made it through the entire service, and she quickly excused herself as soon as the final benediction song began. Rushing down the center aisle to the main foyer, Kenzie asked herself if she was trying to catch or avoid Myles Borden.

It didn't matter. He stood waiting for her, tugging her from the trickle of people exiting the service. The dark blue shirt and gray dress pants he wore were a far cry from the jeans and T-shirt she had grown accustomed to. They were even further from the orange jumpsuit he wore when she first met him. And his hair had recently been cut, trimmed neatly at the back of his neck and off his ears, spiked up slightly in the front.

He blinked once and her eyes settled on his. The blue there

was the same. If everything else about him changed, she would always recognize his eyes.

"Can we talk for a moment?"

She managed a nod only, as her voice refused to respond to her mental commands. But suddenly Nana appeared at her side, clinging to her elbow. Had they been introduced? She could not recall much from the day of Mac's arrest, so she opted to be polite.

"Nana, this is Special Agent Myles Borden. Agent Borden—" Myles's eyebrow arched, most likely in question to her formal introduction "—this is my grandmother, Muriel Thorn."

With a poise that had been ingrained since childhood, Nana held out her hand and shook Myles's. "A pleasure to meet you."

"The pleasure is mine." Myles bowed his head slightly. "Nate speaks very highly of you."

"You, as well." Nana's smile was genuine and her demeanor almost back to normal. "Thank you for what you did for my Kenzie."

Myles never took his eyes off Kenzie as he responded to Nana. "God put me in the right place to protect her. I'll always be glad that God chose to use me in that way."

Kenzie struggled with that thought for a moment. While once she would have trusted that Mac would bring her safely through anything, she couldn't count on him anymore. He'd disappointed her, but God hadn't. He had been there all along, protecting and providing for her through Myles.

And now bringing him back into her life, if even just for a short time.

Turning her attention to Myles, Nana asked, "To what do we owe this visit?"

"I have a bit of news on the case." He glanced around at the small crowds gathering in the entryway. Apparently deciding it was safe to continue in a lowered voice, he said, "FBI agents in Vancouver found Larry Whitestall in a run-down motel yesterday. He sang like a bird about the entire plot, how JB Ryker bribed him to assist in getting rid of you. How they tried to coerce Cory Johns into kidnapping you before they approached me. He even had communication with Mac—"

His voice broke off at Nana's visible twitch, and he quickly altered his word choice. "Larry is going to testify about everything in exchange for a reduced sentence. He told agents that Ryker told him that Mac didn't know anything about killing Kenzie. Apparently, Mac's plan was to have Kenzie kidnapped and scare her enough to never want to return to the prison. He assumed that no one else would be snooping around the budgets for a while. But Ryker decided that Kenzie was too much of a risk, and he ordered Larry to take her out of the picture completely."

Somehow, the news didn't shock Kenzie. Perhaps Mac was almost entirely focused on his position as governor, but he wasn't a sinister man. He could not act like he loved her as much as he had over the years and then sacrifice her so easily. He had wanted to protect her, to keep her out of his underhanded dealings. In a way, even when he plotted her kidnapping, he was still trying to protect her.

But he certainly wasn't the perfect man she had always thought him to be. From the pedestal on which she had placed him as a child and never taken him down, he had disappointed her.

"Will there be any need for Nana or me to testify?" The idea made Kenzie shudder.

Myles shook his head. "It's unlikely. Between the prison budget you provided, the recordings from Mac's office and Larry's testimony, the state has plenty of evidence. I doubt that Mac or Ryker will contest the charges. More than likely, they'll both make plea bargains to reduce sentences at the arraignment in a couple weeks. And with Larry's testimony, the charges of conspiracy to murder against Mac may be dropped."

Nana let out a breath she had obviously been holding. And Kenzie realized she did the same.

"Thank you," Nana said. "Myles, it was a pleasure to meet you. Thank you for everything." She squeezed Kenzie's arm. "If you'll both excuse me, I need to have a word with the pastor."

Kenzie watched Nana walk away, her back straight, head held high. Her silver hair bounced lightly with each step. The dark blue coat she wore hugged her shoulders and waist, giving her the pulled-together look of a governor's wife, even if her husband no longer held the office.

Myles's gaze followed hers, watching Nana strike up a conversation with a man and woman standing next to the pastor. "How's she doing?" His voice filled with genuine concern, he met Kenzie's gaze directly.

"Surprisingly well."

His eyebrows furrowed. "What do you mean?"

"Well, she's really been very understanding toward Mac, but she hasn't made allowances for his bad choices and actions. I think she still loves him. How could she not? They've been married for over forty-five years."

"I suppose."

"But I think she feels like she needs to take care of me, which is understandable, I guess." She shrugged one shoulder, her thoughts suddenly sidetracked by the conservative appeal of Myles's new hair cut. Oh, he did look quite handsome. He always did though, even in orange.

"Kenzie?"

"Yes? Oh! Yes, Nana really is doing well, considering it all.

I think it's a load off her mind that she won't be asked to testify against him."

"How about you? How are you doing?"

Kenzie looked down at her black dress shoes, digging her right toe into the industrial carpet. "Fine, I guess."

This entire situation was so surreal. How could she be having such a calm, collected conversation with this man, when all she really wanted to do was throw her arms around his neck and have him hold her forever?

But the guilt over her own words to Myles kept her from acting on that desire. She had said terrible things to him when he told her the truth. It should not have surprised her that he did not comfort her on the day of Mac's arrest. Likely, he wanted this conversation to be over as soon as possible.

He nodded. "What will you do?"

"Well—"

"Kenzie! I'm so glad to see you here!" Myles jumped back a step at the boisterous greeting from Angela Purdue, one of Kenzie's oldest friends at the church. "I was just thinking about you." Angela's voice dropped to a whisper. "I read about your return and then Mac's arrest in the newspaper. I'm so sorry about everything. Tell me what's going on."

Angela's cold hands clung to Kenzie's, sucking all of the warmth from the room. A shiver ran down Kenzie's spine as she tried to formulate the appropriate response. How did one explain the betrayal of her grandfather because of his own greed, but that she still harbored love for him? How could she clarify that the man standing beside her was both her kidnapper and the man she quite possibly loved?

And like the hero that he always was, Myles stepped forward, put his arm around Kenzie's shoulders and pulled her to his side. "Would you excuse us please?" No explanation, no excuses. He just steered her to a private corner as Angela's face became a mask of confusion.

And then they were alone again. When he dropped his arm from her shoulders, she felt lost at sea. "Myles." She looked at her feet then up to his chin. "Myles, I hate—"

Myles held up his hands to stop her, his stomach falling to his feet. "Save it. I know you hate me. And I'm not assuming that we're going to pick up where we left off. But just hear me out. Please."

"No! It's not that! It's just… I don't hate you. I hate how I treated you. How I acted when you were only being honest with me. I just—I just wasn't ready to hear it. To know the truth."

His jaw dropped open two inches. He closed it and then tried to form words, but no sound emitted from his mouth.

Kenzie reached out to put her hand on his forearm, but stopped about five inches short. His hand sprang out to meet hers, and he held it gently there, hanging between them like the words that he wanted to say.

"Kenzie, I'm sorry," he finally managed to spit out.

"For what?" Her inquisitiveness was genuine as she cocked her head to the side and looked into his face with huge gray eyes.

He stabbed his fingers through his hair, always surprised by its much shorter, more office-appropriate length. "I don't know. Everything. For the prison. For the cabin. For losing your trust."

"You never lost my trust." Innocence shone from somewhere deep within her face.

"Not even when I— When I kissed you?"

"Which time?" She laughed.

He laughed, too. She had a good point. He finally dropped his hand to his side, pulling hers with it, effectively tugging her a step closer.

And then she stepped right up to his chest, whispering words only for him. "Myles Borden, you have nothing—absolutely nothing—to apologize for. You protected me from myself, even when I didn't know that I needed it. You told me the worst possible truth—that Mac loved his position, his power, more than he loved me. I just wasn't ready to hear it." Her hand reached for his cheek and cupped it gently, then slid back to rub the fuzzy hair at the back of his neck, sending a shiver down his spine. "For all my life I've counted on Mac to protect me, to keep me safe. I was afraid to trust what you said, because if it was true, then my safe little world would crumble.

"I was afraid of letting Mac disappoint me. Somehow, I thought that if I refused to believe you, Mac could never let me down. I was wrong."

He could tell she was fighting the urge to look down. Her eyelids flickered, but she maintained eye contact. "I'm sure that someday you'll disappoint me and let me down, like Mac did—well, I hope not exactly like Mac did—but I don't expect perfection from you. I don't need or expect human perfection. It's not possible. But God still got me through this whole ordeal. And He'll get us through whatever lies ahead."

He put his free hand over hers on his neck, holding it in place, relishing the cool feel of her fingers. Having her that close was perfect, like a dream he never knew he'd been longing for. "Ms. Mackenzie Thorn, what am I going to do with you? You were just supposed to be another assignment, another wild adventure. I've been all about my job for a long time, sure that it was where God had me. But you somehow weaseled your way into my heart." He couldn't control his smile as her eyes started to light up. "I thrived on the excitement that belonging to the FBI offered, but somewhere between that mountain lion attack and watching you being held at gunpoint, I fell for you. And somehow, I think that you might just offer more excitement than any job ever could."

"Does that mean that I'm going to be around for a while?" Her innocent smile didn't fool him for a second. He knew Spicy Kenzie was just below the surface, assuring him that a transfer to a desk job within the Bureau wouldn't leave him void of thrills.

"I think you've earned another kiss or two." He chuckled. "I'll have to keep you around long enough to pay up."

She laughed out loud. "Funny. I was thinking that you'd earned a few of your own."

And even though they were standing in the church foyer with members of the congregation milling around them, Myles could do nothing to stop his head as it dipped to press his lips to hers. The others disappeared as he held her close and breathed in her lemon-lime scent. He sent up a prayer of thanksgiving for the amazing woman in his arms.

When voices and conversations around them intruded on their intimate moment, Myles pulled back, just slightly.

"I guess this means that I'll have to ask for a transfer to Salem."

"That seems silly." She laughed.

Doubts bombarded him. What if she did not want to pursue their relationship? Was she just toying with him? Did she think this was the end of what they shared?

Kenzie smiled at the hard look that spread across his features. She flipped a curl of red hair over her shoulder and pressed the hand that he had been holding to the soft cotton covering his chest. "Nana and I are moving to Portland. She needs a fresh start. I do, too. Besides, I've been offered a teaching position at the juvenile detention center there. Maybe if I can help the boys at a younger age, they won't end up in the state prison—like you." She winked at him, enjoying the look of humor reflected in his own eyes.

"I'd go back there to protect you in a heartbeat."

"Really?"

"Oh, yeah," he breathed as he pressed his lips to hers again.

"Well, there are two down for me. How many more have I earned? I'd hate to use them all up."

He threw his head back and laughed. "Oh, those two were free. You'll know when I'm paying up." And deep in her heart she knew that she would have a lifetime to collect on that debt.

* * * * *

Dear Reader,

Thank you for joining Kenzie, Myles and me as we followed the clues to discover the men responsible for the plot to kidnap and kill Kenzie. I had so much fun writing these two characters—especially Kenzie's sweet and spicy sides and Myles's faithful protection.

I'm very thankful that I've never been betrayed by a family member the way that Kenzie was. I have, however, moved far from my family and found that the people I usually turned to during difficult times weren't right beside me. Like Kenzie I had to learn to rely on God and count on His protection and plan for my life. I hope that Myles and Kenzie's story encourages you to do the same when you face trials.

I love hearing from my readers. You can visit my Web site at *www.lizjohnsonbooks.com* and leave me a comment or e-mail me. Thanks again for joining me on this adventure. I hope we have many more to come.

Liz Johnson

QUESTIONS FOR DISCUSSION

1. Who is your favorite character? What aspect of him/her do you most identify with? Why?

2. At the beginning of the book, Kenzie has the opportunity to pursue a different career choice, moving out of the prison and into a kindergarten classroom. If you were in her shoes, would you have made the same decision? Why or why not?

3. At the cabin, Kenzie feels that Lenora both misunderstands and dismisses her fear. When have you felt misunderstood or dismissed? How did you react in that situation?

4. When Myles is attacked by the mountain lion, Kenzie sees that he's willing to sacrifice his own life to protect her. She must decide if she'll rescue him in return. What would you do if you were in this position?

5. Myles gives Kenzie a special gift for her birthday—he celebrates with her. What special gift have you received? What made it so exceptional?

6. In Edna's house, Myles spends his time digging through piles of newspapers, distracted from his ultimate goal by something that appears to be important. What things in life that seem important distract you from God's true purpose?

7. Myles's dream of being a navy SEAL are shattered in high school, which leads him to the FBI and ultimately to Kenzie, God's true plan for him. What goals have you had that didn't come true and revealed a greater plan for your life?

8. When Kenzie discovers that Myles told her the truth about her grandfather's betrayal, she is filled with guilt over the way she spoke to him. Have you been in a similar situation? What was the situation, and how did you resolve it?

9. Mac's betrayal makes Kenzie take a closer look at the way she's put him on a pedestal. Have you ever done that with someone? What happened when they let you down?

10. It's only after both Myles and Kenzie give their broken hearts and their attraction to each other to God that He brings them together for good. What have you had to completely give up to God before He gave it to you?

11. What personality traits do you think Myles and Kenzie have that make them compatible?

12. How has God shown Himself faithful and ever-present in your life, like He did to Kenzie and Myles?

Dumped via certified letter days before her wedding, Haley Scott sees her dreams of happily ever after crushed. But could it turn out to be the best thing that's ever happened to her?

Turn the page for a sneak preview of
AN UNEXPECTED MATCH
by Dana Corbit,
Book 1 in the new
WEDDING BELLS BLESSINGS *trilogy,*
available beginning August 2009
from Love Inspired®

"Is there a Haley Scott here?"

Haley glanced through the storm door at the package carrier before opening the latch and letting in some of the frigid March wind.

"That's me, but not for long."

The blank stare the man gave her as he stood on the porch of her mother's new house only made Haley smile. In fifty-one hours and twenty-nine minutes, her name would be changing. Her life, as well, but she couldn't allow herself to think about that now.

She wouldn't attribute her sudden shiver to anything but the cold, either. Not with a bridal fitting to endure, embossed napkins to pick up and a caterer to call. Too many details, too little time and certainly no time for her to entertain her silly cold feet.

"Then this is for you."

Practiced at this procedure after two days back in her Markston, Indiana, hometown, Haley reached out both arms to accept a bridal gift, but the carrier turned and deposited an overnight letter package in just one of her hands. Haley stared down at the Michigan return address of her fiancé, Tom Jeffries.

"Strange way to send a wedding present," she murmured.

The man grunted and shoved an electronic signature device at her, waiting until she scrawled her name.

As soon as she closed the door, Haley returned to the living room and yanked the tab on the paperboard. From it, she withdrew a single sheet of folded notebook paper.

Something inside her suggested that she should sit down to read it, so she lowered herself into a floral side chair. Hesitating, she glanced at the far wall where wedding gifts in pastel-colored paper were stacked, then she unfolded the note. Her stomach tightened as she read each handwritten word.

"Best? He signed it *best?"* Her voice cracked as the paper fluttered to the floor. She was sure she should be sobbing or collapsing in a heap, but she felt only numb as she stared down at the offending piece of paper.

The letter that had changed everything.

"Best what?" Trina Scott asked as she padded into the room with fuzzy striped socks on her feet. "Sweetie?"

Haley lifted her gaze to meet her mother's and could see concern etched between her carefully tweezed brows.

"What's the matter?" Trina shot a glance toward the foyer, her chin-length brown hair swinging past her ear as she did it. "Did I just hear someone at the door?"

Haley tilted her head to indicate the sheet of paper on the floor. "It's from Tom. He called off the wedding."

"What? Why?" Trina began, but then brushed her hand through the air twice as if to erase the question. "That's not the most important thing right now, is it?"

Haley stared at her mother. A little pity wouldn't have been out of place here. Instead of offering any, Trina snapped up the letter and began to read. When she finished, she sat on the cream-colored sofa opposite Haley's chair.

"I don't approve of his methods." She shook the letter to emphasize her point. "And I always thought the boy didn't have enough good sense to come out of the rain, but I have to agree with him on this one. You two aren't right for each other."

Haley couldn't believe her ears. Okay, Tom wouldn't have been the partner Trina Scott would have chosen for her youngest daughter if Trina's grand matchmaking scheme hadn't gone belly-up. Still, Haley hadn't realized how strongly her mother disapproved of her choice.

"No sense being upset about my opinion now," Trina told her. "I kept praying that you'd make the right decision, but I guess Tom made it for you. Now we have to get busy. There are a lot of calls to make. I'll call Amy." Trina dug the cell phone from her purse and hit one of the speed dial numbers.

Haley winced. In any situation, it shouldn't have surprised her that her mother's first reaction was to phone her best friend, but Trina had more than knee-jerk reasons to make this call. Not only had Amy Warren been asked to join them downtown this afternoon for Haley's final bridal fitting, but she also was scheduled to make the wedding cake at her bakery, Amy's Elite Treats.

Haley asked herself again why she'd agreed to plan the wedding in her hometown. Now her humiliation would double as she shared it with family friends. One in particular.

"May I speak to Amy?" Trina began as someone answered the line. "Oh, Matthew, is that you?"

That's the one. Haley squeezed her eyes shut.

* * * * *

Will her former crush be the one
to mend Haley's broken heart?
Find out in AN UNEXPECTED MATCH,
available in August 2009
only from Love Inspired®.

Love Inspired

HEARTWARMING INSPIRATIONAL ROMANCE

Experience stories
centered on love and faith
with a variety of romances
just for you,
with 10 books every month!

Love Inspired®:
Enjoy four contemporary,
heartwarming romances every month.

Love Inspired® Historical:
Travel to a different time with two powerful
and engaging stories of romance, adventure
and faith every month.

Love Inspired® Suspense:
Enjoy four contemporary tales of intrigue
and romance every month.

Love Inspired®
SUSPENSE

TITLES AVAILABLE NEXT MONTH
Available August 11, 2009

SPEED TRAP by Patricia Davids

The fatal crash was no accident. The only mistake was leaving behind a four-month-old survivor. For the boy's sake, Sheriff Mandy Scott *will* see justice served. Yet Mandy finds herself oddly drawn to her prime suspect—the boy's father, Garrett Bowen. If Mandy trusts Garrett, will he shield her from danger, or send her racing into another lethal trap?

FUGITIVE FAMILY by Pamela Tracy

Framed for murder, Alexander Cooke and his daughter fled to start a new life. A life that brings Alex, now Greg Bond, to charming schoolteacher Lisa Jacoby. Then the true killer returns. This time, Alex can't run. Because now he's found a love—a family—he'll face anything to protect.

MOVING TARGET by Stephanie Newton

A dead man on her coffee shop floor. An ex-boyfriend on the case. Sailor Conyers has murder and mayhem knocking at her door. She'll need her unwavering faith and the protection of a man from her past to keep her from becoming the killer's next target.

FINAL WARNING by Sandra Robbins

"Let's play a game..." Those words herald disaster as radio show host C. J. Tanner is dragged into a madman's game. Only by solving his riddles can she stop the murders. And only Mitch Harmon, her ex-fiancé, can help her put an end to the killer's plans.

LISCNMBPA0709